Paul Sarnet

Summer 1998

A NEW BEGINNING

Fanny Stang

MINERVA PRESS
LONDON
MONTREUX   WASHINGTON   SYDNEY

ISBN 1 86106 317   2

First Published 1997 by
MINERVA PRESS
195 Knightsbridge
London SW7 1RE

Printed in Great Britain by
Biddles Ltd, Kings Lynn, Norfolk

A NEW BEGINNING

In loving memory of my dear husband

Fanny Stang is also the author of *Fräulein Doktor* (1988).
The names of certain individuals have been altered.

Contents

Part One

Part Two

Part Three

Part One

Chapter One

Arrival

The boat train had slowed down and now exhaled a final puff of steam and stopped. I spied through the dark window an illuminated signboard, which read:

VICTORIA STATION LONDON

The young man sitting next to me lifted down my suitcase, shouldered his rucksack, and smiling said, "Here we are."

He was tall, blond and blue-eyed and, though naturally diffident, had entertained me with his holiday reminiscences of his walking tour in the Cevennes – which he had undertaken after reading Robert Louis Stevenson's *Travels with a Donkey*. I had told him in my halting schoolgirl English that I came from Vienna.

"Ah, the city of Johann Strauss and Mozart.". He added with admiration, "You are lucky."

Had he heard nothing of Hitler? How lucky to be so innocent. It was July 6th, 1939, but he had assumed that I was no more than holidaying in England. He had asked no further questions, unaware apparently of Nazis or refugees.

I got up and slipped on my hat with its inevitable Austrian feather, but on looking at my reflection in the window, I decided to take it off. I threw my camel coat over my arm and seized my small pigskin weekend case. The young man lifted my suitcase onto the platform and I stopped him from carrying it any further. He assumed I was to be met.

To my "Thank you, thank you... goodnight..." he replied, "Auf Wiedersehen!" Then he waved and joined the stream of chattering, laughing travellers pushing for the exit. Where to now?

I clutched my weekend case which contained all my documents from birth certificate and school reports to the final glorious Latin text of my MD Vienna. This was somewhat marred by the Nazi stamps which, in bureaucratic German, informed all whom it might concern that I was forbidden to practice medicine in the Great German Reich, which now included Austria. But the most precious of all was my English work permit which had enabled me to come here to take up a position as a nanny and domestic help in a vicar's family in Wallasey in Cheshire.

I looked longingly back at the comfortable upholstered seats in the third class compartment. Third class in Austria consisted of wooden benches. I would not have minded spending the night in such English luxury.

I awoke with a start. A row of beds in front and to the right and left of me. Frightened and confused I sat up – was I in a hospital?

Then it all came back. The emptying station platform, a motherly lady, a ride in a taxi through lighted streets which stopped at a large office-like building: THE SHELTER. A studious-looking young man in an office took my passport, a ride in a lift... Then I must have fallen into bed and slept in my underwear, which would certainly have been frowned upon at home.

My weekend case with its precious documents, my pyjamas and toilet bag stood at the side of the bed. My coat, skirt, jacket and blouse I had thrown over the case, crowning the heap with my hat. The larger suitcase had been stored, I knew not where.

Thin morning light seeped through the tall windows behind me. It must be very early, I thought, and looked at my wrist. No watch! I had forgotten that I had smuggled out my beloved eighteenth birthday watch concealed in a little packet of dates as a *'Liebesgabe'* to friends in Switzerland. Such small 'love-gifts' were permitted by the Nazi authorities, no doubt to show their generosity to the countries abroad. All our other family jewellery and silver had been collected in a house raid by two armed SS men as a 'voluntary' contribution to the building of the 'Third Reich'.

I sank back onto my pillow to the sound of breathing, sleeping bodies. I thought of my parents, probably awake too and worrying about my brother and me. I hoped my sudden departure hadn't brought them more trouble. The notice, delivered in my absence, to visit the *Amt* – probably for the extortion of more taxes, or worse – had spoiled my careful arrangements to accompany a children's transport on the following Sunday. We had fled from the rented flat. My parents transferred to a wretched cheap room, even deeper into the ghetto. I had caught the first train to the coast.

"Don't worry about us," Mother had said.

"Perhaps you will be able to help us to get out, then we could wait together in England to reach our American quota number."

I shifted restlessly and as I turned on my side I saw two dark eyes observing me from the next bed.

"It's very early," the middle-aged woman whispered to me in German. "Go back to sleep. It'll be a long and tiring day."

I smiled to please her, and closed my eyes. But I was now fully awake and thoughts were rushing through my head. Where was my brother now? In a camp, or in a leaky boat somewhere in the Mediterranean? Leo was only eighteen and had never been away from home. Now he was on an illegal transport destined for Palestine. I saw his boat being tossed by the sea making him sick, or wading in the dark onto a deserted shore trying to evade the English soldiers guarding the coast against illegal immigrants.

"Don't worry," Leo had said when I took him to the train in Vienna to join several hundred others. "We have it all carefully prepared." That was back in February. It was now July and still he had not reached Palestine. I stopped this train of thought. I must post a letter to my parents to let them know I had arrived safely. What did English letter-boxes look like?

My head began to ache; after all, I had not eaten for thirty-six hours. I opened my eyes and looked at my friendly neighbour. She was sleeping but not deeply as her eyelids were twitching. I thought longingly of my iron rations – the slabs of plain chocolate in my case, packed by my mother. I shifted carefully onto my back and drew my stomach muscles in tight. I was longing for somebody to stir so that I too could get up.

At last one dark head surfaced from the sea of breathing bodies at the end of the dormitory. I dressed swiftly and joined her.

At breakfast in the basement refectory, I sat with my neighbour at the long table. I swallowed some of the bitter tea provided in large teapots – it was my first taste of Indian – and took a big bite of the buttered slice of white bread.

"Herr... I didn't catch the name... is very arrogant. Never wastes two words when one will do!" said the dark-haired, long-nosed girl, curling her thin lips in disapproval as she leaned across the table to speak to my neighbour.

"I think he is simply shy," she observed.

"At least he speaks perfect German," the grumbler returned grudgingly.

"And I heard him speak French equally well," my kind neighbour added, before turning to me. "You are from last night's batch," and, looking at my cup which was still two thirds full, she continued, "I can see you're not used to strong English tea."

I was about to apologise when she pointed to the white jug and sugar bowl. "Add some milk and lots more sugar."

This I did and smilingly acknowledged the improvement.

"Are you from Austria?" I nodded, my mouth full.

"You will need to register. Do you know where to go?"

"No," I stammered. "Is it far?"

"Not very far. I always walk; it saves money and you get to know the place. Would you like to come with me?"

I accepted gratefully.

I returned tired and hungry. It was late and the dining hall was deserted. Somebody had covered the long table with a white sheet and Sabbath candles were lit, spluttering at one end.

I suddenly realised that it was Friday evening. Mother would have lit the candles and would be worrying about me. I should have sent a telegram but then a telegram nowadays always meant bad news. I tried to console myself with the thought that my postcard would be delivered on the following morning.

Looking into the dying flame of the last candle in its pewter candlestick, I remembered other Friday evenings; the gleaming damask tablecloth, the tall silver candlesticks, and the candlelight dancing in the breeze of an open window; Father at the head of the table humming a Sabbath hymn, his blue eyes smiling. He adjusts his black skullcap on his fading blond hair and carefully pours red Tokay wine into four wine glasses. Mother sits on his right in her customary Friday night white blouse. Her black, gleaming hair is arranged in a neat Eton crop, brushed high over her forehead. Her great dark eyes scan the table as she adjusts the salt-cellar for the blessing of the bread. My brother, sitting by her side, opens his prayer-book; his cheeks glowing, he brushes an obstinate brown curl under his skullcap. My place is to the left of Father and I surreptitiously sniff at my well-scrubbed hands to be quite sure that I have eradicated all scent of the dissecting room. Father rises and we follow. He lifts his glass and says the blessing over the wine. "Amen".

But no warm glow of home pervaded me here. The candle had wept its last waxen tear and extinguished the flame. I ladled the half-congealed noodle soup into my plate. I then devoured the meat, the soggy peas and potatoes of institutional cooking, washing it all down with black tea. It was a strictly kosher meal, so there was no mixing of meat and milk.

How Mother would have enjoyed seeing me clean my plate without pickings and leavings, I thought, as I kept heaping sugar into my glass of tea. It still tasted bitter. How different from the mild Russian (China) tea at home; but this did not stop me from defiantly drinking the witch's brew.

That first day I had walked all the way from Whitechapel to Bloomsbury House – which was known to the initiates as the 'Vatican' – and back. No flags, no swastikas; young friendly faces, many men in khaki uniforms; very tall policemen with funny high helmets and business men in dark suits, bowler hats and exquisitely rolled umbrellas – although there was not a cloud in the sky. The girls wore pretty flowered dresses and everybody seemed so amiable that I smiled and they smiled back.

I was now an officially registered refugee from *Grossdeutschland* and the possessor of a little blue book – a 'vade mecum' for refugees. It bore my name and the number A15355 on the first page.

I settled down at the end of the long dining table to study all twenty-four pages – English on the left side and German on the right. This was to be my first exposure to English literature in this country.

On the stiff midnight-blue cover I read: 'while you are in England' and, in thick black capitals:

HELPFUL INFORMATION AND GUIDANCE
FOR EVERY REFUGEE

After five pages of lists of useful organisations, I was told how to register with the police (this was to be done within three months of arrival) and how to appreciate the sympathy felt towards refugees here. Some cardinal points on suitable behaviour were set out:

Spend your spare time immediately in learning
the English language.

Further on:

> Don't speak or read German in public; better
> halting English than fluent German!

I quite agreed. I never wanted to speak German again. I was determined to acquire fluency in my hosts' language as soon as possible and I started by reading the entire text in English only.

> Do not talk in a loud voice. The Englishman greatly
> dislikes ostentation, loudness of dress and manner.

Good, I thought, I don't like them either!

> You will find that he says 'thank you' even for the
> penny ticket for which he has paid.

And finally:

> The Jewish Community, which bears all expenses
> for the refugees, is relying

and the next part in thick black print:

> ON EACH AND EVERY ONE OF YOU
> TO MAINTAIN DIGNITY AND SERVE
> OTHERS WHEREVER POSSIBLE.

It concluded:

> BE LOYAL TO ENGLAND, YOUR HOST!

I wondered whether it was really necessary to remind us of our positions; after all, my *own* country was bent on destroying us.

My hopes were raised by page twenty:

> The Home Office would favour immigrants
> who could establish businesses and offer
> employment to British workers.

I promised myself that I would explore this matter. My parents could certainly do this, and then we might be able to settle here!

I then turned to the inside of the back cover where a helpful table of English money, weights and measures was available for study. It seemed a very cumbersome system, but, obeying the little blue book's injunction, I suppressed my critical thoughts and read it carefully. Four farthings equalled one penny, and twelve pennies equalled one shilling. A two-shilling piece went by the musical and romantic name of a 'florin'. Two shillings and sixpence was a 'half a crown'. Twenty shillings were one pound. Twenty-one shillings went by the odd name of a 'guinea'. Yet I looked in vain for a whole 'crown'.

My head was reeling. I postponed the weights and measures table for careful study at another time.

Chapter Two

Maurice

On Saturday, Bloomsbury House was closed, but I was busy trudging along London's streets to carry out commissions I had been given by friends in Vienna, mostly letters and messages. I was also anxious to find a cheap room for the one or two weeks I intended to spend in London, exploring possibilities for my parents before I started on my job in Cheshire.

I had a letter for Rosa, the daughter of friends of my parents. She had a room in Arthur Street, off Upper Thames Street. I consulted my map and turned towards the river on leaving the Shelter in Mansell Street.

The shops were closed for the Jewish Sabbath. I passed men in dark suits and trilbies, who were obviously going to the synagogue. A few with beards and sidelocks wore the fur hats and silk caftans adopted by our ancestors in Poland and Russia.

It was still early, but already quite warm under the cloudless sky. I found my travelling suit too hot so I shed my jacket and slung it over my shoulders. A pleasant breeze caught me as I neared the river. The long terraces of three and four storied houses, often with shops on the ground floor, added to my impression that a host of villages had amalgamated to become this great city. A cart laden with huge beer barrels, drawn by a pair of immense dray horses, proceeded at a sedate walking pace, almost blocking the narrow road.

I emerged to see the battlements of the Tower of London. I tried hard to remember the history connected with it, but it evaded me, except for a vague memory of two pathetic little princes done to death.

At last I came to London Bridge and stopped to look over the parapet at a large number of ocean-going ships. As I watched the swaying masts, I wondered whether one would carry me to America.

How small the Danube seemed now! Beyond it my parents were marooned in a ghetto room in the second district. Father would be at the local synagogue, or what remained of it after the destruction during the *Kristallnacht*. Mother would be alone, sitting at the table with the burnt-out candles in old bottles left untouched from the previous night. Not to be removed until the first star marked the end of the Sabbath. She would be reading and re-reading the account of my safe arrival. Behind me, two soldiers passed by and I thought, 'On Monday I shall start trying to get you out of that rat-hole.'

When I enquired at the house in Arthur Street, Rosa's landlady informed me that she had gone out. I decided to leave the letter and scribbled my shelter address on a slip of paper. I had two more commissions which I kept for the afternoon and turned back to the Embankment. I found an empty bench and sat down to munch the bread and butter sandwich I had saved from breakfast.

I looked up into the blue sky above the dancing masts and made a covenant with God: if He helped my parents to get out safely, I would keep all the religious laws and rites at whatever cost and effort it might involve – there were six hundred and thirteen of them according to Maimonides.

On Sunday afternoon I went to see Dora Spitz, a colleague who was to receive my mail until I had an address of my own.

Today Hessel Street market was alive with people. The shops were open and fish tanks fronted the street displaying carp and other fish. They swam around lustily, ignorant of their fate. Shop entrances were flanked by barrels of salt herring and pickled cucumbers pungently scenting the air.

I turned left this time towards Aldgate. As I passed the handsome stone pump, I wondered if water would still flow if I pressed the handle. I was reminded of Dr Snow who had, at some time in the past century, removed a pump handle somewhere in London and stopped the spread of typhoid in his district. The typhoid bacterium had not yet been discovered, but observation and an inspired guess had led the doctor to the correct conclusion.

Ah, when would I be able to return to medicine again?

I consulted my map for the London Hospital and discovered that I had to proceed across Commercial Road.

Dora had failed her finals in those hectic months after Hitler's invasion. She had emigrated at Easter on a domestic work permit and was employed as a ward maid at the London Hospital. As I entered through the glass doors I spotted her. She was wearing a pale green overall and her dark fringed hair was completely covered by a white cap, like a nun's. She was at the far end of the hall carrying a tray of crockery.

"Dora! Dora!" I cried.

She turned and smiled in recognition, but shook her head and continued on her way.

I went up to the reception desk and was told that she would be off duty soon, during 'visiting time', but I was permitted to wait. Visitors began to arrive and suddenly a bell sounded and they all hurried along to the wards.

Then Dora came towards me. She had taken her cap off and was waving two letters at me. She hugged me as she explained that she was not allowed visitors whilst on duty. We huddled together in the privacy of a broom cupboard and she encouraged me to open the letters.

Mother's first words were to take care of myself. She said that they were 'all right'. I breathed a sigh of relief as I told Dora of my sudden departure. The second letter contained a pencilled note from my brother – Leo had reached Rhodes and was waiting for a ship with a captain greedy enough to run the British blockade and take him, and several hundred other illegal immigrants, to Palestine.

I dropped the letters into my handbag to be read later at my leisure; then I could decipher the hints and secrets floating below the surface.

We exchanged news. Dora was hoping to join her brother in New York and resume her studies. Her parents, like mine, were waiting for their American quota number to be reached. She gave me the address of a Jewish family in the East End who had a spare room to let, assuring me that it would be cheap.

On the way back I passed some young soldiers with kitbags and rifles. A disturbing sign of mobilisation. It started to drizzle and I hurried to reach the Shelter. I was once more almost the last at dinner.

I swallowed my food and settled down to re-read my precious letters. Then I wrote to my parents and my American uncles. By the time I had finished and had returned from the friendly red pillar-box, it was quite late. Noticing my soiled white cuffs, I realised that I had not changed my blouse since my arrival. My suitcase had been stowed away somewhere in the basement, so I went to the office to find out where.

I faced the young man who had taken my passport on arrival. He looked up from his book, but I found I didn't know the English for 'suitcase' and stammered, "I can my... *koffer*... not find."

He smiled and replied in excellent German, "You may speak German to me if you like."

"I shall never speak German again!" I retorted defiantly.

"Very well," he replied, "but in that case you will have to learn better English. Come along and I'll help you to find your suitcase. I've finished in the office."

I suddenly realised that this was the 'arrogant Herr Shtang', the subject of the discussion at the breakfast table on my first morning.

We descended into the storeroom. My case was lying on top of a great pyramid of luggage and was quickly recovered. I opened it and extracted a bar of my iron ration of plain chocolate called 'Bittra'. Maurice – I had already learned his first name – commended its quality. We sat down on the steps and talked while we munched the chocolate.

It was long after midnight before I got to bed.

Next morning, true to his promise, Maurice was in the hall as I came up from breakfast.

His brown hair was still wet from what I suspected to be a hasty application of soap and water to keep it tidy. It was tightly brushed down over his high forehead. A long multi-coloured scarf brushed the floor and his light brown Harris tweed jacket strained at the buttons. It was the first time I had seen him in the daylight.

In his early thirties and overweight, I promptly diagnosed. I strongly disapproved of his bulging pockets. I later discovered that one held several bars of Cadbury's milk chocolate and the other a stubby volume of Immanuel Kant's *Kritik der reinen Vernunft* (*Critique of Pure Reason*).

He looked down at me through silver-rimmed glasses. His hazel eyes made me feel a warm glow of happiness. I pushed aside the feeling, suddenly smitten by guilt. How could I enjoy a man's company with my parents stranded in the Viennese ghetto and my brother in some leaky tub on the high seas!

Last night, sitting on the steps with my suitcase beside me, eating plain chocolate, I had confided my hopes and worries to Maurice. We had debated the possibilities for myself and my family until the early hours. Now we set out for Bloomsbury and walked and talked as if we had known each other for years. We spoke English and only interspersed the odd German word when my knowledge fell short.

I insisted on calling first to see the room Dora had mentioned. It was nearby in a side-street, a dark, dirty and dismal place.

"Thank you," Maurice said. "It's not quite what we had in mind." He bowed slightly to the landlady as he gently touched my elbow to steer me out of the house.

"You needn't be in such a hurry. I can find you a more suitable place."

We skirted the river, walking along Eastcheap, Cannon Street and Queen Victoria Street. One could sense the river's presence even when it was out of sight. Maurice stopped in front of the Foreign Bible Society.

"As a schoolboy," he explained, "I used to buy fourpenny portions of the Old Testament in exotic tongues, which I construed with the aid of an English Bible."

I liked walking, and so did Maurice. It was the only way to get to know a city, we agreed. At the beginning I found it irksome to adapt myself to my escort always walking on the gutterside of the pavement and not on my left as in Austria. I learned that in England a lady was always 'given the wall' and the reason – I was shocked to hear – was that slops used to be thrown into the street as late as the eighteenth century. When we crossed the road at an orange Belisha beacon, Maurice put his hand lightly under my elbow to guide me. I would have liked to take his arm, but felt too shy.

"That's my Alma Mater," he pointed out as we passed King's College in the Strand. The entrance was squeezed between a tailor's shop and a public house. I was taken aback by so uninspiring an entrance to a university college. Yet, looking through the courtyard, I could see classical columns facing the Embankment.

"How strange to screen this beautiful building with shops and a... *wirtshaus*!" I stammered, though reluctant to find fault.

"You mean a 'pub'," he corrected. "But the college also has a fine chapel. I must show it to you sometime."

"Anyway, at least there aren't any stairs to throw you down," I commented, still smarting from memories of my university experiences in Vienna. There, Jewish students had been beaten by Nazis and thrown down the beautiful flight of stairs of the Greek facade. When they arrived, bleeding, on the pavement, they were arrested as troublemakers.

On reaching Bloomsbury House, I called at various offices armed with information gathered from the little blue book and my discussions with Maurice.

"My parents could start a clothing factory here," I stated confidently. But this fell on stony ground as I was unable to prove that they had sufficient funds. Our money (actually, it was my dowry) had been transferred – at a price – in a diplomatic bag to my uncles in America.

Maurice waited patiently for me while he read Kant. Each time I emerged dispirited from an office, he fed me chocolates and consolation.

In the next office I tried using another ploy: "My parents have affidavits for the USA and are only waiting for their immigration quota numbers to be reached. All they need is a transit visa to wait here."

The officers were very sympathetic and it seemed to me that I merely required documentary proof. I was elated and told Maurice I would write to my uncle that very night.

By now it was midday. Maurice stood up and said, "Now we will take one of our beautiful red buses, which you must learn to use, and go to a famous and strictly kosher restaurant for lunch."

"I want... to walk..." I hesitated, hindered by my poor command of English.

"Why walk? It's the same way we came!"

"I want to save money," I stated, shamefaced.

"I am paying!"

I still hesitated, but he went on, "In this country it is awfully bad manners to refuse when you are invited by a friend, *sehr unhoeflich*," he added, in case I had not understood the English expression.

"But..." I ventured.

"But me no buts – do you know that expression?"

"No," I admitted. He smiled and, touching my elbow, steered me firmly out of the building. "You see, you have a lot to learn. But I will teach you in no time," he added reassuringly.

We went to Bloom's in Whitechapel. I devoured half a roast chicken, while Maurice hardly touched his.

I neatly arranged the knife and fork beside the denuded skeleton.

I had a vision of my parents sitting in their miserable rented ghetto room waiting for post from me and my brother.

"We will get your parents out – if only the war holds off," Maurice said, although I had not voiced my thoughts. He laid his hand on mine and was about to say something when the waiter appeared to remove the plates. He withdrew his hand and asked me to choose a sweet from the mouth-watering dishes on the menu; but I felt guilty and ashamed of my greed. So we finished with lemon tea.

We returned to the Shelter, Maurice to his office and I to write letters.

That night I slept without nightmares.

Chapter Three
The British Museum

I awoke refreshed and hurried through my breakfast to get to the office to see if any post had arrived for me.

In the hall, I found Maurice waiting for me, waving a letter. Nervously, I tore it open and a pencilled note from Leo fell out. My brother was still in Rhodes. A fire in the engine-room of the ship in which they had left Rhodes, two days earlier, had forced them to return. No one had been hurt, though, and he asked me not to worry. They were hoping to board another ship soon.

The letter from my parents reassured me that they were well and that their only concern was for my brother and myself. I was to call on Mr Landesmann, an old friend of our family, who had arrived from Switzerland and who had greetings for me from our friends there. He was staying at Tavistock Square.

On our way I changed my precious £10 cheque, a gift from the Rothschild Hospital for six months' voluntary work. The cheque carried a grace and favour permission from the Nazi government to export it. I deposited the sum of nine pounds and ten shillings in the Post Office further down the road, and retained ten shillings for emergencies. The balance would have to keep me for the duration of my stay in London.

As we passed St Paul's, Maurice pointed to Wren's beautiful dome. "It was built after the Fire of London in 1666, which destroyed the Gothic church. Don't you think London is a beautiful city? You must not leave it."

The lovely baroque architecture reminded me of Vienna.

At Tavistock Square I learned from my newly acquired mentor that London had spread westward in a series of squares built during the eighteenth century. The clay for the handsome brick houses had been dug on the sites themselves. These excavations, in the course of time, were turned into small, elegant parks.

"I'll wait for you here." Maurice sat down on a bench and drew out a slimmer volume than usual.

I walked across to the house and lifted the heavy, brass lion's head knocker. The reverberation that followed sounded forbiddingly hollow. How strange, I thought, not to have a friendly bell. An elderly lady opened the door.

"Herr Landesmann is *leider* out, but he left this for you," and she handed me a letter and a little box marked '*Vorsicht*'.

"*Danke*, thank you," I corrected myself and scribbled a note on a page torn from my address book. I thanked the lady again and hurried back.

I knew what was in the box marked 'Take care' and was eager to show it to Maurice.

Absorbed in his reading, he did not notice me crossing the square. He smiled and lovingly stroked the page before turning it over. He only looked up when I stood in front of him. For the moment I forgot the box in my handbag, distracted by his absorbed and tender handling of his book.

"What are you reading?"

"Heine's *Buch der Lieder*," he replied. "*Book of Songs*, you know," he added, smiling, imitating my corrections into English, whenever I had inadvertently used German words. "I admire his poetry very much."

"You know the Nazis burnt his books?"

"Of course," he replied.

Remembering the surprise that nestled in the bottom of my handbag, I sat down. "I want to show you something I have just collected from our friend."

He closed his book and carefully slipped it into his pocket. I extracted the matchbox and slid out the contents wrapped in cotton wool to reveal a very small gold watch and matching gold strap.

"A present from Mr Landesmann?" he asked, astonished.

"You might almost say so," I laughed. "No, not really. He just collected it for me from our friends in Switzerland. It's the watch I was given by my parents on my eighteenth birthday."

I then explained about the Nazi policy of allowing a *'Liebesgabe'* to be sent abroad, presumably to demonstrate their liberality. Only chocolates, figs and dates, of course. Strictly no money or valuables.

"So, how did you get a gold watch through?" Maurice asked.

"Ah, that's where my dissecting skills came in! I carefully unwrapped a packet of dates, removed the stone of one, placed the watch inside and fitted the edges together. Then I repacked the whole thing and sent it with birthday greetings to our family friend Herr Heller. When he sent a letter, which he often did, adding his thanks for the birthday gift, I repeated the operation in another packet of dates and enclosed the strap. A week later the Gestapo collected all that remained of our valuables."

"So you are a little smuggler!" he laughed.

"Yes. It took Hitler to make my father tolerate such immoral behaviour," I sighed. "I only wish I could get my parents out as easily."

"You will. Look! There is the BMA, the British Medical Association – and, if you should stay in this country, it will be your future trade union." He got up and continued: "Now, let me show you my real university." And he led me to the British Museum.

As we mounted the steps I admired the magnificent portal and immense columns. Two silver lions' heads on either side of the entrance were spurting drinking water into handsome Grecian silver goblets secured with long chains.

"Real silver!" I exclaimed.

"Silver-plated, probably."

"And nobody steals them?"

"There are porters watching!" Maurice commented, seemingly unimpressed, but my esteem for this country had risen to new heights.

"The Reading Room is straight ahead, but as you found the Berlin one so impressive, we'll visit the Egyptian collection today."

"It was the head of Nefertiti that I admired so much."

We passed the Rosetta Stone and I learned all about its significance for the deciphering of hieroglyphics. We walked on past the giant heads of the godlike Pharaohs. Suddenly my eye was arrested by a limestone sculpture: a man and a woman seated on a stone bench. Unlike the gods and kings they were of normal size and displayed human affection as they sat there holding each other's hand for all eternity. I looked at the inscription; the pair were from Thebes and belonged to the eighteenth Dynasty circa 1350 BC.

"When you marry me, we will sit side by side like these two ancient Egyptians and walk through life holding hands. I love you!" he whispered into the top of my head, pressing a kiss on my curls.

I looked up into his smiling hazel eyes and knew we had sealed a lifelong bond.

For the next two weeks I continued my visits to Bloomsbury House collecting information. Maurice was always at my side.

Chapter Four
Meeting the Family

Some two weeks later Maurice took me to his home to meet his mother.

We left the 159 bus in Brixton Hill Road. This still retained something of its Victorian suburban affluence: long, narrow gardens led to the semi-detached three-storey houses with tall bay windows and roomy basements.

"Once these were middle-class family homes with kitchens and sculleries in the basement and servants' quarters on the top floor," Maurice explained. "Now most of them have been converted into flats."

Tall plane trees separated each pair of houses from the next. Half a dozen steps led up to the front doors, which were decorated with colourful leaded glass.

"These gardens are like the parks in Vienna with their carpet-like lawns and neatly cut hedges," I commented.

Maurice unlocked the door of number 13 and drew me into the cool, well-lit hall. To the right was a tall staircase and to the left two doors. The front room door opened and an old lady emerged.

"Meet my mother," Maurice smiled.

I was surprised, she looked much older than I had anticipated and reminded me of my own grandmother, who had cuddled me as a child. Her untidy grey hair framed a lined, care-worn face, resembling the portrait of an old woman by Rembrandt that I had recently seen at the National Gallery. She was my height and her sad brown eyes lit up as she raised them to look at her son.

"This is Fanny, a refugee from Austria," Maurice introduced me and added, "She is a doctor." His mother looked me up and down.

"A doctor?" she murmured incredulously as she slowly raised her hand to shake both of mine, which were extended in a warm greeting.

"I am so glad to meet you, Mrs Stang; how kind of you to invite me to your home." I had carefully prepared what I considered to be the most English sort of greeting. My engaging smile met an astonished look and I suddenly realised I had not been expected.

Maurice did not allow me to linger but drew me into the next room, his bedsit study. His mother did not follow us.

It was a high-ceilinged, square room with a large bay window overlooking the garden. To the right of this was a rolltop desk above which was a glass-fronted bookcase. Facing me was an enormous marble fireplace which could easily have accommodated a small tree trunk. It was flanked by two open-shelved bookcases filled to capacity. In the bay stood a large, square table, covered with an oilcloth usually found in kitchens, and surrounded by several straight-backed chairs. Maurice told me that as a child he had done his homework on a kitchen table covered with an American oilcloth cover and retained a superstitious belief in its efficacy for good work. Notepads and books were strewn over every available surface, including the sofa-bed to the right of the door.

"Ready for tea?" Maurice did not wait for an answer. "Find yourself a seat and I'll get my mother to make us some."

"May I look at your books?"

"Of course, take your pick: German, French and even English."

As I turned to watch Maurice walk out through the open door, I noticed his mother standing just outside weighing me up. I turned back to the books, but then it struck me that I should have offered to help his mother with the tea. I took two steps and then stopped in my tracks. I could hear Maurice's voice: "Fanny is going to stay with us..."... mumble... and then Maurice again, quite clearly, "I am going to marry her." Mumble, mumble... and then his mother spoke up, "... but there is nothing of her!"

I caught sight of myself in the long mirror of the three-doored Victorian wardrobe to the left of the door. She was quite right: I was five feet tall and weighed less than seven stone.

Maurice returned and stood behind me, looking over my head into the mirror. His outline formed a dark frame against the reflected window. He wrapped his arms around me and I felt enveloped in tenderness and love.

"I hope your mother will like me," I whispered.

"Of course she will!"

"I realise I am taking her only son from her."

"And she is getting a wonderful and precious daughter!" He laughed. "What a cliché! 'Wonderful', 'precious' – these are hackneyed adjectives and you must never use them."

I didn't know what 'hackneyed' meant, but felt I'd got the gist of its significance.

"You must understand," he spoke seriously now to my mirror image, "my mother and her family came to England in 1911 from a small village in Latvia. Three of her brothers were tailors. Her eldest brother, a teacher, had stayed behind and was killed during the Bolshevik revolution. He fought for the Tsar! The men were artisans while the women bore children, cooked and gossiped. Life was hard but simple." With this, he turned me back into the room and said, "Stop worrying, you are marrying me, not my mother. Come and look at my philosophy section. We shall read Hegel together, or perhaps we should start with Aristotle or Plato."

"I haven't read much philosophy, except for Nietzsche's *Zarathustra*, and I don't think I quite understood that."

His mother appeared with a brown earthenware teapot, milk jug, sugar bowl and two cups and saucers on a tray which she deposited somewhere among the books before returning to the kitchen. A moment later she brought in a plate of chocolate cream buns.

"Fresh from the milkman this morning," she murmured. At her heels a large black cat stared at me and bared his teeth in disapproval.

"We will need some hot water. Fanny isn't used to English tea yet."

"Can I get it?" I volunteered.

"No." His mother held up her hand in refusal.

"Your mother is not having tea with us?"

"No, she has her next door neighbour in for a teatime gossip."

After depositing the hot water jug, Mrs Stang withdrew, the cat at her heels, and closed the door behind her.

Maurice seemed quite unperturbed and I soon forgot the episode as we talked of Georg Büchner, the German revolutionary playwright, and the subject of Maurice's MA thesis.

The following week, Maurice took me to meet his father, who owned a small factory in a three-storey house in the East End. The upper floors had previously been inhabited by the family. The large workroom on the ground floor was crowded with sewing machines, ironing boards, and along the walls were shelves filled with roll upon roll of cloth and bundles of fur.

His father looked surprisingly young and agile. His blond, slightly curled hair framed his clean-shaven face, and his blue eyes smiled at me.

There were several young men at the machines and a number of girls were tacking garments by hand – 'felling hands', I was told later.

"My father is an exceptional tailor and one day you must get him to run something up for you."

His father took my hand in both of his, gave me an approving smile and said, "My son has good taste." He invited me to look around and showed me some chinchilla furs which he was preparing to trim into a collar for a coat. His informality made me feel, more than words could, that I had been accepted into the family.

The following day we were invited to lunch by Fay, Maurice's sister. She lived in Trent Road, a ten minute walk from his home. Their small, black Morris car stood in the road opposite her green front door. Maurice lifted the shining brass knocker above the letter box slit. Fay opened the door immediately.

"Come in, come in." She extended a warm hand in welcome. She was my own height, but with a fuller figure, and her dark brown straight hair was cut short to frame her round glowing face. She wore horn-rimmed glasses which enlarged her brown eyes.

Showing us into the front room off the hall, she said warmly, "I shall only be a few minutes; I have to see to the meal. Please make yourself at home."

The oval dining table was covered with a white damask cloth set with silver cutlery. Four glass bowls contained pale green grapefruit halves with sugar melting on the top and a red cherry in the middle of each.

I looked curiously at the open sheet of music on the upright piano to the right of the door. It was 'In a Persian Garden'. To the left, against the wall, a glass-doored display cabinet housed two tall silver candlesticks and the best china tea service. A comfortable settee and two armchairs stood in the bay window. A small sideboard next to the fireplace seemed to fill the room.

Fay returned to put some dishes on the sideboard. "Isaac will join us in a moment. He's just finishing some business with a customer." I had been told that he had a tailoring workshop in the back room.

It was a warm, domestic atmosphere and made me feel uninhibited and happy.

Chapter Five

Brixton Hill

"It's time you saw the secretary of the British Medical Association and got some information about your medical studies," Maurice said as we returned to the Shelter.

"Is my English good enough?" I asked nervously.

"Good enough for the purpose. I shall take you there tomorrow."

"Don't I need to make an appointment?"

"My friend at the London Hospital assured me that you don't. Dr Macrae is a very kind man."

Next morning I gathered together my Viennese MD, with glowing reports from my Professors – all complete with English translations, duly supervised and corrected by Maurice.

"You are sure I don't need an appointment?"

"Now calm down, I'm quite sure he won't bite you."

Maurice took me up to the impressive portal in Tavistock Square. "I'll wait for you on a bench over there." He pointed to the park in the square and watched as I went inside.

In the waiting-room a receptionist took my name, which I carefully spelled out for her: K–N–E–S–B–A–C–H. I discovered there was a man and woman in front of me and a trickle of newcomers followed. Each time the office door opened a kind-looking man shook hands with the departing colleague and called out for 'Dr Nisbatch'. As nobody answered to the name, the next 'Dr Smith' or 'Dr Jones' was invited in. When I was the only one left we discovered that he had been calling my name all the time, leaving out the 'kn' as in 'knowledge'.

I entered his office and in some confusion sat down in his chair. After the usual niceties were exchanged, Dr Macrae put me at my ease. We later became great friends and he put up with my repeated visits, always ready to help.

On returning to the Shelter for my last night there, I sat down on my bed in the empty dormitory, eager to write home and tell them the good news – and, indeed tell them of all that had befallen me. I slipped my writing pad out of my case and retrieved my fountain pen from my bag. It was then that I noticed the still unopened letter from the morning post, forgotten in the excitement of visiting the British Medical Association. Impatiently, I tore open the envelope. It was a reply from a trusted colleague and old friend in Vienna whom I had taken into my confidence.

> *Highly esteemed Fräulein Doktor,*
> *Your letter was a pleasant surprise, but the contents shocked me and I reply in haste.*

My heart started to beat a rapid tattoo:

> *You tell me you are in love and are contemplating marriage with a man you met barely three weeks ago!*
> *Well, I am not surprised he has fallen in love with YOU and wants to marry you in great haste, for you possess good looks and an endearing and loveable personality! But just consider, you are in a strange country, your appeal is enhanced by your need for assistance; he is kind and eager to help you. Don't mistake your feelings of gratitude for love on your part!*

"Gratitude doesn't come into it!" I shouted at the page.

> *I shall, of course, not mention any of this to your parents, but they will have to know soon – unless you change your mind! And remember: better a little hardship now than a life of misery in a marriage founded on a momentary infatuation! Take your time!*
> *All in the hospital send their best wishes – I have, of course, not hinted at any of the above to anybody – this is our secret for as long as you wish it.*
> *I am proud to have been taken into your confidence in this matter.*
> *Your ever devoted friend,*
> > *Arthur*

My eyes filled with tears. Would my parents feel the same? I blinked away the tears and read the letter again. It reminded me of that Friday evening when I announced that I was going to study medicine. Father and his friends were all against it. I was right then and I am right now, I decided defiantly. Unscrewing my fountain pen, I wrote:

> Dear Mama,
>
> I hope that Father's hand is better and you won't have to do all the writing.

But then I hesitated – 'Why add to their worries!' I thought, and continued:

> You will be glad to hear that Mr Stang's mother has invited me to stay as a guest in their house.
>
> Since his sister got married and lives in a house of her own, her previous bedsitting room is free.
>
> The house is a tall family home – what we would call a 'villa' – built at a time when families were large and servants plentiful. Now the top floor and the basement have been converted into flats, and Maurice and his parents occupy the ground and first floors.
>
> Mrs Stang reminds me very much of Mama's mother. She is overweight and although only in her fifties, she looks much older. She has kept to her house and garden for the last four years. I am sure she needs a medical check-up.
>
> Now you and Papa need not worry that I'll break the dietary laws, for I am to eat with the family as their guest.
>
> I can stay in London with a clear conscience as I have heard from Wallasey that I can easily be replaced. I shall now look for a job here. From tomorrow I shall be at my new address. I have an appointment tomorrow afternoon with Mr Roth, in room 110 at Bloomsbury House, in connection with your visa. The gentleman was recommended to me by our friend, Mr Landesmann. I feel there is a change for the better coming for us at

last.

Lots of love and kisses from your loving daughter,

Fanny

I sealed the letter and wrote my new address on the back of the envelope.

'Better to let them come here first, meet Maurice and then they will see that I was right to marry him.' Thus I consoled myself for the deception.

Back came a letter by return of post.

Dearest Fanny!

Your letter of the 27th gave us great joy. We had a really happy Sabbath as we received at the same time a postcard from Leo in Rhodes in which he says he hopes to soon be on his way. He has found an acquaintance who has promised to help him.

I am enclosing Mr K's letter. It does not sound promising regarding your application to do research at the University in Jerusalem. His wife is still here. What a fate to have a strange woman of the same name receive her visa by mistake!

We are glad that you are now looking for a job in London. Papa doesn't think you would have made a very good domestic help!

As for us, don't worry so much, we are all right. Keep in touch with Uncles Sali and Karl in America, and with Leo when he reaches his destination. We pray to God it may be soon.

Please convey to your hosts our joyful thanks and best wishes for their kindness to you. We hope one day to be able to thank them in person.

Love and kisses,

from your parents.

PS Papa's hand is not too bad, but he is feeling sorry for himself so I am spoiling him a bit.

After the weekend break, I did manage to speak to Mr Roth and at last success seemed to be within my reach. I made a list of the documents needed and joyfully sat down to write:

Dear Parents,

I have spoken to Mr Roth at last and he promised to process a transit visa in four weeks, if I can get the necessary documents to him.

I wrote to Uncle Sali a fortnight ago to let me have copies of the affidavits. I need from you both a short curriculum vitae, copies of birth, marriage and health certificates, passport photographs – all, of course, authenticated by the USA Consulate in Vienna.

I am writing this in my room by the open window, looking out onto the back garden. It is a beautiful day; the sky is blue and cloudless and all the gardens here are ablaze with rose bushes. A blackbird has just settled on the bird-table. The black cat is snaking through the grass towards it. But she shan't get the bird.

If only you could be here at my side... but I must hurry to catch today's post collection. I want you to start getting all the papers together as soon as possible. Lots of love and kisses,

Fanny

I thought of the front room next to mine furnished as a double bedroom. I won't say anything yet, but with new hope I hurried, letter in hand, to the post office in Brixton Road to ensure its speedy despatch. On the way back I even allowed myself to daydream about how Maurice and I would collect my parents at Victoria. Yes, we would be extravagant and take a taxi all the way back.

Next morning the following letters reached me. One was from my uncle in Chicago and another from Zurich.

Dear Fanny,

I have taken immediate steps to get copies of the affidavits, which is not too easy as I did not keep copies at the time.

We hope all goes well for you in London.

There is a great deal of unemployment here and your Uncle Karl in New York is having quite a hard time of it, especially as your aunt is expecting her baby in a month.

Your aunt and cousins all send their regards,
Your loving Uncle,

Sali.

I passed the letter over the breakfast table to Maurice and opened the second one.

Esteemed Dr Knesbach!

I am so glad to hear that you have settled at last in London; that you are in good health and living with friendly hosts. I know that you must be unhappy that your dear parents are still in Vienna.

However, your father has only himself to blame. I advised, and indeed begged him, last summer to send Leo out of the country. I told him every time we met that our young people should leave. When I got to Zurich, I wrote to him of various ways to get out. Why didn't he go to Belgium and from there to Italy? I have even sent him an invitation from an Italian family.

Now that you can write to me openly, how does he stand with his immigration to America? What does the future hold for you? Please write and tell me all the details – I am very concerned about you all. My son is leaving on the 9.9 for America. My other children there are not doing too well.

My wife and I hoped to travel in November, but our affidavits were found not to be in order and the police here now are very strict and totally without. mercy. A young man committed suicide because he was being deported back.

It is very terrible! May God help us all!
Regards to you, your parents and Leo,
Your friend,

Moses H

I pushed the second letter over to Maurice. The kipper, now my favourite English breakfast dish, no longer held any attraction; I slid it into the cat's dish under the table. The cat always ate with us and waited patiently for the leftovers. Although curled at Maurice's feet, he accepted food graciously from any source.

I took a few sips of tea and watched Maurice's expression.

"I'm sure if my parents could have gone to Belgium, they would have done so," I said. "As a jeweller, Moses had long-standing business connections with Zurich and Antwerp. He doesn't appreciate the obstacles that exist for people without connections there."

"Yes, of course," Maurice replied thoughtfully.

"I remember well how at the beginning he promised to pull some strings for us. Each time we found a letter with a Swiss postage stamp in the letter box our hearts would pound with anticipation. Each time it was just good advice."

"It's your uncle's letter that troubles me." Maurice had taken it up again. "He doesn't sound very keen to see you there. Are you thinking what I'm thinking? Unemployment in the USA, no copies of the affidavit kept, and will they be found in order?"

"Yes, you're right," I sighed. "If the copies are not here when my parents' documents arrive, I will ask for the five thousand dollars to be transferred. Then I can deposit the money in my parents' name to prove that they have private means here."

It was Sunday, the 20th of August. I woke from a restless sleep to a chorus of birdsong and a silent house. The drawn curtains over the large, slightly open window admitted a shaft of sunlight and a gentle breeze.

For a moment I felt confused. Then, once again, I was seized by those now obsessive thoughts – I must write that letter I had postponed for so long.

Yesterday, Maurice had registered our marriage for the 9th of September – his birthday!

"When your parents get here, we will have a synagogue wedding to please them," he said.

Neither of us was in the mood to even think about the pomp of a religious ceremony and a showy wedding reception.

Getting up, I slipped on my red flowered dressing gown and drew the beige rep curtain. Grey mists hung like spider webs between the shrubs. Dewdrops glistened where the struggling sun rays struck them. Reluctantly, I turned away from these morning glories and sat down at the oval table in front of the window.

Last night I had set out my writing pad, fountain pen, envelope and stamps. Now, to ensure that I had a full pen, I unscrewed it, pushed the plunger into the bottle of Stephen's blue-black ink, readjusted the pen and wrote:

Dear Parents,

A large blot prevented me from proceeding. I wiped the pen on the blotter, tried it, and then started on a new sheet.

Dear Parents,
I have great news for you...

No, that wouldn't do. I tore the page up. They might think before reading any further that I had miraculously received the entry visas, even before receiving their documents. I started again.

Dear Parents,

Please try and hurry up the documents. I am told if all goes well they could be cleared within four weeks for visitors' visas.
Now I have some great news for you...

But this is nonsense! Of course they are hurrying as much as they can. Had I forgotten that they would have to make appointments for medical examinations, authenticate copies at Embassies and so forth?

Getting up, I walked over to the window and pushed up the sash. Below, in the garden, noisy sparrows accusingly circled the still empty bird-table and settled on nearby branches to wait. Our black cat spotted me as he looked up from the bottom step of the kitchen. A gentle though firm 'miaow' floated up as a reminder that he too was waiting for his breakfast. A breeze sent rolling waves through the tall grass.

And where would Leo be now – probably in some ramshackle boat trying to evade the mighty British Navy?

(I was unaware that at dawn that very day my brother had in fact waded ashore near Haifa.)

Another more insistent 'miaow' reminded me that Maurice's mother would soon be up to feed us all.

Then Fay, his sister, and her husband would be calling for us in their little Morris to take us for a picnic on the beach in Brighton. This was to be a special treat to show me what an English Sunday by the seaside was like. Maurice had groaned about the ordeal, but submitted to it for my benefit.

How happy I would be, if only I could get my parents out of that hellish ghetto room in the Komoedianten Gasse – that unreal world. They wouldn't even be aware of the feverish preparations for war here: conscription, blackouts, gas masks, air raid shelters. I was unable to mention any of it as letters could well be censored.

I heard a door shut below and stirrings from above. I must write that letter. Yes, I shall urge them to consider the invitation our friend Heller had mentioned from Italy. I would then tell them that although Maurice and I had known each other only a short time, we had fallen in love from the moment we met and had yesterday become engaged.

I wrote the letter and sealed it, determined to post it without further heart-searching.

Chapter Six

The Reading Room

Two days later, when Maurice and I set out on our routine trip to town, a newspaper poster caught my eye.

RUSSO–GERMAN PACT OF NON-AGGRESSION

And sitting in the tram, we overheard a city gent in front of us say to his colleague, "It would be suicidal for us now to back the Poles."

"Do you think Chamberlain will say the same?" I whispered to Maurice.

"I suppose we'll have to fight them in the end, but this may delay our intervention."

Maurice was still a committed Communist and he thought it reasonable for Russia to delay before entering the war. His experiences in Spain in the International Brigade had taught him the necessity of being well prepared for war. He was, however, convinced that Communism would finally defeat Fascism and bring peace to the world. But he was horrified and withdrew his membership when the Communist Party of Great Britain immediately declared that British intervention against Hitler was not in the interests of the Proletariat.

On that day, however, he had his mind set on far more personal problems, as any delay would give me time to get my parents out. For this reason, I allowed myself to enjoy the journey on that swaying tram, hurtling down Brixton Hill Road, plunging at the Embankment into the underpass at Southampton Row, to emerge a few yards from the British Museum. All this for the price of a fourpenny return ticket. (They made excellent bookmarks: they were one inch wide and four inches long and they still turn up in books we were reading at the time.)

Maurice had introduced me to the British Museum Reading Room, for which he had held a ticket since his university days. I had boldly declared my field of scholarly research to be 'The History of Medicine' and, sponsored by Maurice, I made my application and secured the magical piece of pasteboard which opened the door to this Aladdin's cave.

We entered the vast circular Reading Room, with its long lines of desks arranged like the spokes of a wheel. The morning sun came in veiled through the tall rounded windows above the tiers of bookshelves.

Picked out by a ray of sunlight, a lone attendant on the third tier was collecting a pile of books.

We passed the black figure of the Abbé Leclerc, who filled his ample black armchair and looked as if he had been there all night. In the weeks to come, I was to see him in the same posture, the same seat, the same pile of books to the left and right of his desk space. He sat compiling, single-handedly, an encyclopaedia of Catholic antiquities. He didn't pause for lunch, but discreetly swallowed a sandwich and took a gulp of brandy – both heinous crimes, but in his case generously overlooked by the authorities.

In J8 I spotted another of my regular landmarks: Miss McDonald, wearing white Bermuda shorts and plimsolls, sitting in the seat where once Lenin was reputed to have sat.

"She's a classical scholar but writes unreadable novels. She cycles from Hampstead and is first in the queue at nine every morning, awaiting the opening of the Reading Room." Maurice obviously admired her punctuality more than her scholarship.

I must ask him where Karl Marx sat, I thought.

Then I spied the free seats in the D's and made straight for numbers six and seven, which we had occupied yesterday. We deposited our bags and handed in our slips for our reserved books. We needed only to enter the new date. I handed in the tickets at the central desk and within minutes a friendly attendant brought the slim volume of Singer's *History of Medicine* and the two tomes of Gray's *Anatomy* and Boyd's *Pathology*.

I found the footstool provided for small people's comfort and settled into the massive wooden armchair, generously moulded to encase the human body. This was the most comfortable chair I ever sat in and far superior to its upholstered successors.

I relaxed in the hushed atmosphere of the muffled footsteps of the attendants delivering the books, occasional whispers, and the scratching of those steel pens still provided at every seat. Thus breathing the cool air redolent of old books and scholarship, I opened Boyd's *Pathology*. At odd moments I peeped into Singer wherein I found many old friends. I was delighted to read that Lister knew and appreciated the work of Semmelweiss at the great Viennese maternity hospital where I had trained.

Maurice had a growing stack of nineteenth century German books on his desk as he gathered material for his MA thesis on Georg Büchner. He never seemed to need to look at a dictionary, while I found myself writing out columns of English words I didn't know. I had always hated looking up dictionaries and now I had my own living work of reference sitting next to me. I loved the tender way he handled books. His fingers turned the pages as if he were playing the strings of a delicate instrument.

At lunch-time we walked out and sat on the benches under the colonnade to devour our sandwiches with a Heinz spread, and drink coffee from our thermos flask. The meal was spiced with discussion about our work.

We returned for another hour or two, then handed in our books at the centre table to be reserved for our use the next day.

Maurice departed for his office in the Shelter, and I went home to do some shopping in the huge Brixton market. I took the tram straight back and consulted Mrs Stang about any items she might want, memorising exactly what she said and where to get it. What she mysteriously called 'clod-o-ly' was understood by the saleswoman at the hardware stall and correctly supplied to me as a bottle of 'chloride of lime' (a domestic cleaning fluid). My favourite shop, however, was the large Woolworth's on the main road. No English was needed. I pointed to the desired articles, the salesgirl supplied it and I paid the carefully marked price. The items were either threepence or sixpence.

Before preparing supper, I wrote out an essay for Maurice to correct when he returned. He would always read it while eating the light meal I had prepared for him. This might be at two in the morning sometimes.

Next morning the first of a succession of letters arrived in reply to my announcement of our engagement.

22.8.39

Dear child,

Your letter has greatly surprised us. In fact, we couldn't believe our ears – such a very hasty decision from our sensible and cautious Fanny!

Of course we wish you and your dear fiancé the very best of good fortune. May it be a blessing for the whole family. We only pray, dear children, that you will not be in undue haste to marry, so that the joy may be granted to us of leading you under the wedding canopy.

Shortly after receiving your letter, Mr Maier visited us and told us that it was true that the 850 people who landed in Haifa on Saturday and were interned, included the group from Constanza. We now hope to hear from Leo soon.

We will send you our papers tomorrow or at the latest on Friday. Do all you can to speed up our visitors' visas.

Please tell us more about your future in-laws and send us photographs. Does Maurice have any brothers or sisters? Are they all English?

I wanted to write you a much longer letter but we are still stunned by yours, so I am unable to think straight.

Am I correct in concluding that the engagement was on Sunday 20th of August? Enough for today.

Love and kisses,

We hope to see you soon!

Your loving parents.

PS Special regards to your fiancé, his parents and family as yet unknown.

PPS Remember, dear child, that you promised us to run a kosher home one day when you embarked on your medical studies, seven long years ago.

'Yes, I shall remain kosher and keep all the laws, if only you reach England safely.'. I vowed this again.

Next day the documents arrived and I immediately took them to Bloomsbury House. I was told that there would be no news for at least four weeks. Once more, I wrote telling my parents to try to get out of Austria as friends had suggested, perhaps to Italy. This was followed by two further letters at two day intervals.

Dear child,

We just received a letter from Leo in Haifa, saying that he was well and had landed last Sunday. He thinks he may have to stay for two or three weeks in the camp.

Shall we despatch the crate of furniture to your address?

About your engagement – we are still speechless! Our little girl, and such a quick decision for one's whole life! That you had not said a word about it, all this time, is something we find it hard to understand. Have your present circumstances prevented you from writing to us? Or are you really sure that this young man is your free choice? Have you any information about him? What is his profession and will you be able to live in decent circumstances? Have you told him about Uncle David? Have you perhaps merely done this for our sakes?

Dear child, these are not reproaches but queries. You know how our trust has been betrayed during the last few years. That is why I beg you to explain! In the end, perhaps, you may have been destined to find your good fortune by journeying to London. May you both be very happy together. Amen!

We are in good health,

Love and kisses to you and Maurice

from your parents.

PS I had a lovely dream this week which I will tell you about in my next letter.

I read and re-read the letter. I must assure them that Maurice didn't want to marry me for the money our uncles held for us in America, and that I was not selling myself for British citizenship. I then tried to describe our love for each other. I filled four pages and took the letter straight to the pillar box.

Dear Fanny,

Your letters of the 23rd, 25th and 8th have reached us today. I still can't understand you. You have been only seven weeks away and you ask us why we don't leave. To leave we need an exit visa and an entry permit, and neither can be easily obtained.

Regarding the crate of furniture – for the last week we have been unable to do anything. About your suggestion in your letter of the 25th, we are unable to decide.

Finally, we are now fourteen days before the High Holidays, which will be another month gone. By then we hope that if you exert yourselves we may be able to join you.

May God give us peace all over the world. Your reasons for haste, dear children, are insufficient to deny us the pleasure of leading you under the wedding canopy. I have, dear Fanny, taken enough trouble with your upbringing to deserve this joy.

Now, my dears, we are not in the mood to write any more today. We remain with love and kisses your affectionate parents, living in the hope of a happy reunion.

Chapter Seven

A War Wedding

That Sunday morning, Maurice and I were sitting side by side in front of the open window at his work table. His pen-holder, its Waverley nib dipped in red ink in eager anticipation, was poised above my latest essay. I remembered the advertising jingle Maurice had taught me in praise of his favourite nibs:

They come as a boon and a blessing to men
The Pickwick, the Owl and the Waverley pen.

But I had my reservations about pens dipped in red ink. His fountain pen, filled with sombre blue-black for his own writing, lay neglected on one of his fourpenny notebooks. A huge pile of British Museum book slips, secured by a rubber band, rested beside it. My lesson began:

"You can't…"

But my mind was not on my work. I was still in a euphoric mood after Mother's postcard the day before.

30. Aug. 39

Darling Fanny,
I really must tell you that we have just received our very first letter from Leo. Imagine, four days after landing he was able to visit Mr K in Haifa. He is well, thank God, and enthralled by the Land of our Fathers!
I wanted to share this moment of happiness with you.
Love,

Mother

I looked up at our rolled-up black-out blinds (acquired from Woolworth's) and prayed for just three more weeks of peace. 'Please, it isn't that much to ask!'

On the previous evening a heavy thunderstorm had lit up the sky, and reminded me of past holidays in the Austrian Alps. Now a fine scent of roses and damp grass wafted in through the window which overlooked the back garden. Our local silver barrage balloon hovered above the trees like a giant plump silver bird. Above it, swan-white clouds drifted slowly across a blue sky.

Mrs Stang had just put the remains of the breakfast toast on the bird-table and returned to the kitchen, with her black cat at her heels. Distant church bells mingled with the excited twitter of the birds descending for their meal.

Suddenly, I heard the voice of our French lady from the basement flat, shouting, "Madame Stang, Madame Stang! Chamberlain has declared war!"

"Maurice, did you hear that?" I jumped up and dashed next door.

"I have just heard him say it on the wireless," she continued, as she excitedly climbed the cast-iron stairs from the garden to the kitchen. "Oui, c'est la guerre!"

She had been to Mass that morning. She now deposited her black leather handbag, gloves and coquettish small straw hat on the mantelpiece, straightened the white lace collar of her sombre black silk dress and patted her bobbed brown hair which had been waved with knife-sharp precision.

Mrs Stang mechanically put the kettle on for their morning coffee and chat, while I stood there paralysed, leaning against the doorpost. Madame Duval turned to the open door and shook her fist at the blue sky.

"Les sales Boches! Le bon Dieu will punish you!"

As if in answer, the hysterical wail of the air raid siren rent the silence. Our black cat raced in from the garden and cowered under the chair. In his fright, he had even forgotten to bare his teeth at me.

Mrs Stang sighed and proceeded to pour the coffee. She took a cup and some biscuits on a plate into her son's room, straight past my frozen figure. Returning, she handed me a cup of coffee.

The 'all clear' sounded almost before I had drunk my coffee. There was an almost audible release from tension. Madame Duval and Mrs Stang settled down to more mundane gossip and I returned to

Maurice. He sat there, deep in thought, his coffee untouched. He turned as I swallowed a sob and sat down.

"What am I to do now? I won't even be able to write to my parents!"

He put his arm around my shoulder and I buried my face against his chest.

"We'll communicate by way of your friends in Switzerland and Holland, and of course, there are your uncles in America."

"All our plans have collapsed! I am so afraid for them!" I whispered.

But I cheered up the next morning when I received a reassuring letter from our friends in Antwerp.

> *My father and I are in close correspondence with your parents. We have sent them an invitation to come here and hope they can take it up. The money your father kindly lent us is at his disposal.*
>
> *We were filled with joy to learn that your brother has landed safely. May God help us all to reach our goals soon.*

On the way out that morning we added to our equipment two buff-coloured cardboard boxes. They contained our gas masks. The 159 bus came before our usual tram and it dropped us off at Trafalgar Square. Everybody that day appeared to be carrying a gas mask.

When we passed the National Gallery we saw men loading large wooden crates onto waiting lorries, no doubt full of precious paintings. There was a similar scene at the Museum.

Carefully, we picked our way between the sandbags and the red fire-buckets crowding the corridors. The Reading Room, however, was reassuringly its old self. Studious heads were bent over notebooks and other readers stood at the high central desks, leafing through the giant catalogues. Our diligent Abbé was seated, with piles of books to the right and left of him as usual.

When we left, Maurice turned eastward to his office, while I stole an hour book-browsing in Charing Cross Road, a pleasure unknown in Vienna where the book shops kept their books sealed from the public's touch. I hurried to Foyles, where I had found and was reading a second-hand copy of Vicki Baum's *Unfall In Lohwinkel* (*Accident in*

Lohwinkel), and sat down on a handy stool. I felt sinful reading German – we never spoke the language, although Maurice worked with German books all the time. We always discussed his work in English. However, Vicki, after all, was a refugee just like me. I promised myself that one day I too would write, but in English. I thought I was young enough to make the switch from my native language. I limited myself to one hour's indulgence before making my way to the bus stop. One more visit and I would finish the novel.

On the Brixton Road I called at the post office and drew out two pounds and ten shillings to get the wristwatch I had spotted at the jewellers for Maurice's birthday. When I got home I showed it proudly to Mrs Stang.

"Oh, he never wears a watch. He could have had a gold one had he wanted one. He'll not wear it!" Such was her discouraging comment.

On Friday morning, we returned together to buy my wedding ring for thirty shillings. The smiling attendant threw in a handsome bone-handled cake knife. This was to be our only wedding present – and we still use it to this day.

Saturday morning dawned, warm and sunny, and promised to be a fine summer's day, even though it was the ninth of September. I dressed in my midnight-blue silk suit, which had small pink squiggles printed on it, and matched it with a pink, short-sleeved georgette blouse. I brushed down my unruly curls and put some lipstick on. Then, on second thoughts, I wiped it off again. I was not sure: did one kiss at a Registrar's wedding? Taking my blue handbag, I went downstairs.

Maurice wore a navy blue lounge suit instead of his usual Harris tweed. We drank some coffee, but neither of us wanted anything to eat. I was glad that it would be the simplest possible ceremony and was comforted by the thought that all I would have to contribute was to say 'yes!'.

The Registrar's office was within walking distance.

Half a dozen steps, sprinkled with confetti, led up to the heavy wooden doors. A bride, all decked out in white, was descending the steps. A bevy of relatives were laughingly throwing confetti over a groom in army uniform as he followed her down to the waiting photographer.

At exactly 11.30 by Maurice's new birthday watch, which he wore in spite of his mother's prediction, I climbed the steps between him and his father, who had been waiting for us. On Maurice's left was Ken, his comrade in the Spanish Civil War. They had both crossed the Pyrenees in rope sandals by a smuggler's route.

The youngish Registrar, in a black suit, stood behind his desk. At first, because of the thumping of my heart, I did not take in what he was saying until he turned to me. I then found, to my astonishment, that I had to repeat after him certain formulas in Shakespearean English, including the antiquated 'thee'. In my excitement I repeated the end of a sentence, "I marry *THE*, Maurice..." We were not invited to kiss.

Suddenly it was over. We signed the big book, as did our two witnesses. The Registrar, smiling his complicity, informed me that it was the bride who kept the 'marriage lines'. So I clutched the precious document and we turned to leave just as another couple mounted the steps.

My father-in-law pressed what seemed to be a large, neatly-wrapped bar of chocolate into my hand. Then, after wishing us good luck, both our witnesses departed. We climbed on a bus to the West End for our wedding breakfast at Kettner's in Wardour Street. By then it was quite hot and when I felt in my bag, the softness of the 'bar' that had been slipped into my hand made me feel anxious.

"I think the chocolate your father gave me is melting."

"Chocolate?" Maurice asked in surprise, as he squeezed my shoulder. "I am the chocolate man in our family. Let's see what it is!"

I tore one end off and we found it to be a neat packet of crisp pound notes, fresh from the bank.

Maurice laughed. "A ring, a cake knife and a bundle of pound notes – the best of omens and most practical of wedding presents!"

Part Two

Chapter Eight

Married Life

"Good morning!" I said to my mother-in-law as I entered the kitchen. She sat at the table, dressed in an old cardigan over her flowered summer dress.

"Hmm!" she mumbled. Her breakfast of salt herring and buttered black bread, brought by my father-in-law from the East End, was laid out before her. She sipped her tea. Her familiar lifted his yellow-green eyes from his saucer of milk under the table and bared his teeth at me in a disapproving 'miaow'.

"I'll take our breakfast up. Maurice worked very late last night."

"Ah, poor boy," she sighed as I put the kettle on the gas stove and began to set out our breakfast tray. "And what are you giving him for his breakfast? What, no tomatoes, no cheese, no eggs! Take him some of this lovely herring, at least! Poor boy! He is studying day and night and not eating properly!"

I looked out into the garden to consider my defence. It was a brilliant October morning, the sun just catching the dewdrops on the leaves and the lawn.

"Well, there *is* cheese and tomatoes and eggs... ah, I'm afraid there is only one egg left. I'll boil that."

'I am not going to bicker on a lovely morning like this,' I decided.

"Oh, my poor boy, he is too good; he won't eat it if you haven't got one too." More sighs. "And what are you giving him for dinner – something nice?"

"Well, I think I'll buy some plaice... " And to please her I tried to show off my newly learned skills, "which I'll fry, and we'll have chips with it... and cauliflower or cabbage," I added, seeing in her eyes the unspoken question: is that all?

"How can you eat cabbage with fish? It's unheard of! Impossible!"

"You are right. Cauliflower... and we'll finish with stewed apples and custard," I said hastily. Then, trying to change the subject: "Would you like some fresh tea?"

"This old brew is good enough for me." There was a pause as she watched me cutting the loaf.

"You cut the bread so thin!" she criticised. "I never bother how it looks – I cut good thick slices. I'd give him twice as much as you have here for both of you, and two eggs, and lots of lovely things and..." she sighed "... he used to leave it! Now he is so hungry that he eats it all. Ah, poor boy. And what will you have for supper?"

"I haven't thought about it yet."

Her silence betokened a criminal lack of foresight; but the kettle was singing my release and the egg was ready too.

"Oh, poor boy, how he used to eat and what he gets now!"

I escaped upstairs with the tray to my old bedsitter which we had converted into our bedroom. Maurice woke as I entered.

"I have missed you," he mumbled. Then, when he opened his eyes and saw the tray, he grinned. "You are spoiling me. What will my mother say?"

"She has just told me that I am starving you. Now, sit up and have your egg before it gets cold."

"What, only one egg? We'll share it."

"Don't be silly! You must eat it all."

"Well, decapitate it with your usual skill while I pour the tea and we will have spoonfuls each."

I couldn't resist telling him of the interrogation regarding his welfare that I had just suffered.

"Worse than an anatomy exam!" I said. We laughed and ate.

"I think it was all this food that drove me to Spain to be starved by Franco and live on donkey meat and chick-peas. You should have seen me then! But back at home I was soon fattened up again."

"Now your wife is starving you, 'poor boy'!"

"I shouldn't worry if I were you."

But I *did* worry, for I wanted my mother-in-law to like me. I knew that, with her Russian-Jewish background, my minor reforms in Maurice's diet truly alarmed her. I wanted to improve her own regime, to enhance her general state of health, to smarten up her appearance and to get her to go out occasionally. It was my bounden duty, since I had filched her only son. So far, however, I had had little success.

I decided to do something that my mother-in-law would surely appreciate. Every time she opened the front door she grumbled about the overgrown hedge, all forty foot of it. The young man who had regularly trimmed it had joined the army. Maurice spent every spare moment working on his thesis or on my English lessons. So that afternoon, when he had left for the Shelter (which was now being closed down), I decided to tackle it myself.

I had never used a pair of garden shears, but I had watched a neighbour at work, who made it look like child's play. I found I had to stand on our wooden steps to reach the top. However, it was very hard work to get an even cut and it was quite dark when I finally finished. I was very tired and aching all over, but trusted in my mother-in-law's forthcoming approbation to compensate me for the blisters and aches. I was fast asleep before Maurice returned late in the evening.

Next morning my arms and back had seized up and Maurice went down to bring our breakfast. That in itself was another black mark against me.

"You are a fool to waste your time and energy on a hedge. But I love you!" he added as he massaged my aching limbs and shoulders with the patent liniment he had found in the bathroom cabinet.

Late in the afternoon, when I crawled out of our bedroom, I heard our char's loud voice in the hall, "... My old man would have called it a right cock-up. Who's done that bloody hedge?" A mumble from my mother-in-law was followed by, "Ah, them foreigners!"

Was it praise or blame? Impatiently, I consulted the Concise Oxford Dictionary, but the definition of a male bird, and all the other combinations, made no sense. When Maurice came home he enlightened me with the warning not to use vulgar expressions! Thus ended my career as a gardener.

In the space of six short weeks, I had failed in housekeeping, cooking and horticulture.

However, there was one person in the house who had confidence in my abilities.

Mrs Harris and her husband lived in the two-roomed flat on the top floor. I was surprised to learn that her husband was eight years younger; he was of stocky build and by profession a wrestler. It was a bad time for such work and I once saw him in tears when he returned home after having been paid only five shillings for a bout. He was always behind with the rent and made up for it by doing any odd jobs around the house. He adored his wife and tried to make life easier for her by shopping and running errands for her.

Mrs Harris was a cheerful, middle-aged woman in her final month of pregnancy.

"My fifth, and I hope it is a girl." Her four boys had been evacuated to her parents in Yorkshire. "I knew Peter would want to be with me at the birth so I stayed behind with him in London." She ran her hand through her short brown hair and smiled. "I must have a fresh perm – it will never do to receive my daughter in such a state." She hesitated. "And I am going to have my baby at home. I had my first one in hospital and from the start he was more trouble than the other three put together. Never again!" I must have looked surprised because she added in explanation, "Yes, my GP didn't like the idea at first."

'Of course,' I thought – 'the fifth, non-contracting uterus, post partem haemorrhage,'. I shuddered at the thought.

She continued, "... but I booked a domiciliary midwife and showed her that I had suitable facilities. Mind you, I don't really like her but I'll manage." She added in a conspiratorial whisper: "I don't know why, but I haven't taken to her. Some people you take to, others you don't!"

A week later I was preparing the breakfast when Peter came dashing downstairs.

"My wife has started! I'm going for the midwife. Will you watch Joan for me, please!"

I hurried upstairs, but I had no intention of doing more than hold her hand and whisper soothing words.

Mrs Harris smiled bravely at me as I entered her bedroom. It had obviously been competently prepared. A washbasin stood at the bottom end of the bed, full of steaming water. Brown wrapping paper covered the bottom sheet. The top sheet only partly covered her drawn up knees as a contraction drew drops of perspiration onto her forehead.

"Don't push!" I shouted. "Breathe deeply and relax when it's over." I wiped her forehead with the towel she had laid ready to hand.

However, the contractions were now following each other in quick succession. Where on earth was the midwife?

"Deep breath, Mrs Harris, please!" I almost pleaded.

"It's no good, she's on her way – you'd better take a look. I think she will be out with the next one."

I looked and, to my horror, there was the dark, hairy, shiny occiput. No time to wash my hands or get a clean apron. I wrapped the towel around my waist, abandoned all my Viennese drummed-in hygienic precautions and, recalling the instructions, took over.

"All right, one push; take a deep breath as I rotate the head." The contraction over, I cleared the baby's mouth of mucus with my unwashed index finger. "No more pushing!" I helped the right shoulder out and the left slipped free followed by a gush of amniotic fluid with the rest of the baby. A lusty cry greeted us as I lifted the squirming little body onto her mother's deflated abdomen.

"Yes, it's a girl," I laughed. "How did you know?"

"I just did." She smiled and raised her head to look at the squealing shape of waving arms and legs. "Is she all right?"

"I think so," I answered guardedly.

"I wanted *you* to deliver her. Thank you. I shall tell them at home that she was delivered by a Viennese doctor!"

Then it struck me: I could be in trouble! Barred for ever. Headline in the Daily Mirror: "Unqualified (or was it unlicensed) refugee delivers baby"!

"Better say nothing, please."

"Not here, of course not."

It was then that we heard the midwife's car crunch to a halt on the gravel drive. Even before the second car door slammed Mr Harris was in the room. I felt the still pulsating cord and wished I could tie it and disappear – but there was nothing I could use.

"It's a girl!" Mrs Harris exclaimed, laughing at her husband. "Just as we'd hoped." Still panting from his climb, he bent over and kissed her. A quick look at the baby and he hurried into the kitchen.

A breathless, overweight midwife now appeared in the open doorway. Her eyes swept over the scene. She took a deep breath, straining the button on her blue uniform blouse.

"So, you did a BBA on me," she said accusingly to the happy mother, dropping her bag onto the chair by the table.

Out came a bottle of Dettol. In an instant she had poured some into the washbowl and cleaned her hands. Now the room smelled right. She gave me an encouraging smile and said: "Hold on, dear, I won't be a minute." I went on pressing the now limp cord between thumb and index finger. On went a white starched apron and she unrolled her instruments wrapped in a white towel.

"One would have thought with your fifth, you would know when to send for me!" she grumbled.

Mrs Harris smiled and winked at me. "This one was so quick, I hardly had time to prepare the bed."

Mr Harris came out of the kitchen with a baby bath and a kettle of steaming hot water. I stood there, frozen, not daring to move or speak.

"Thank you, my dear." The midwife turned to me and then to Mrs Harris. "Lucky your neighbour was here!"

Released by the midwife's clamp on the cord, I nodded and slipped out of the room, rushing downstairs to wash my hands.

Maurice was brewing our tea in the kitchen. "Congratulations!" he said. "Your first English medical case and a successful delivery." He laughed when I voiced my concern at not being qualified to practise in this country. "It was an emergency," he reassured me. "Even the dustmen would have been thanked for helping."

'It's true,' I thought, 'anybody could have done that delivery.'

Mr and Mrs Harris were very happy with their daughter. Mrs Harris left two weeks later to join her family, and Mr Harris enlisted.

Years later I learned that 'BBA' meant 'Born Before Arrival', a much disliked entry in the records of any domiciliary midwife.

Chapter Nine
Maurice Enters War Work

Encouraged by Maurice, I was teaching myself typing and shorthand from a Gregg's manual.

"It will come in handy for lecture notes," he said.

I had neatly typed the application for a vacant post at Bateman's, the opticians, to test vision and fit glasses. I even got an interview.

"You need a special certificate to qualify for the job," I was informed by the manager. My MD didn't count.

The drughouses, where I was prepared to do anything, wouldn't even look at me. And when, much to Maurice's disgust, I applied for a private nursing job, I was defeated by death overtaking my patient before I had a chance to start.

Thus a neat pile of letters of rejection was amassing on my corner of our large work table.

I often looked despairingly at the impressive letter-heading of the Scottish Conjoint Board on my first application:

Royal College of Physicians of Edinburgh

Royal College of Surgeons of Edinburgh

Royal Faculty of Physicians and Surgeons of Glasgow.

That was my desired goal, but the letter itself read:

Aug. 1939

Dear Madam,

I have to thank you for your letter of the 10th inst., and in reply have to say that the number of foreign graduates to be admitted to the examinations of this Board has been restricted to seven per annum and that, in the meantime, there are no vacancies.

I am,
Yours faithfully,

David Thomas.

The signature had been stamped and my name misspelt.

A fortnight after my marriage, I went again to see Dr Macrae at the British Medical Association. He congratulated me and was happy to change my name on his list. Furthermore, he wrote to the Scottish Conjoint Board on my behalf to confirm that I was now a British subject and firmly intended to remain in this country. But the Edinburgh quota for graduates of foreign universities still applied to me. Nevertheless, I was invited to apply again the following year. Kindly Dr Macrae tried to encourage me with, "We'll need all the doctors we can lay our hands on... ultimately."

But even all these failures were far less painful than my inability to help my parents. Letters now had to go via our friends in Zurich and Antwerp. My brother, too, had no permanent address and collected his post from friends in Haifa and Jerusalem. He bravely wrote me not to worry, that he was earning his living and was all right. His only concern was the plight of our parents. He had heard that the Jews still remaining in Vienna were being sent to camps in Poland. He was going to pray at the Kotel (Wailing Wall) on the forthcoming Yom Kippur, the Day of Atonement.

I too fasted, feeling at one with my parents and my brother, and Maurice joined me.

After the first few weeks in September, our gas masks remained secure in their boxes at home. There had been occasional air raid warnings, but they were mostly ignored, except by the wardens.

As October faded into November, the efficiency of the blackout increased and badly needed white lines were painted down the middle of the roads. Twice a week we went to our local cinema. We had three within ten minutes walk from our home. Munching tuppenny bars of Cadbury's chocolate, we followed the instalments of 'Andy Hardy' with Mickey Rooney, and entered gratefully into the fantasy world of the *Wizard of Oz* with Judy Garland. English propaganda films aimed to raising our morale by showing German pilots turning back in craven fear at the sight of our barrage balloons. On the wireless, Lord Haw Haw told us of the Nazi successes.

If the sirens sounded during a performance, the manager would stop the film and offer to return the ticket money (one shilling or one and sixpence) to anyone who wanted to leave. But few patrons left at this stage of the war.

When I first learned from Maurice that the performances were continuous, I insisted on seeing each film through twice while Maurice sat patiently by my side. The first session gave me the bare bones of the story, but the second time round I could really follow the dialogue. It taught me to master connected conversations between English persons. I was tempted sometimes to sit through a third session, but was too ashamed to suggest it.

At the end of October, I received an elaborately printed invitation from my uncle in Chicago to his daughter's wedding reception at the Sherry Hotel, 1725 East Fifty-third Street, – RSVP. In the accompanying letter he complained of hard times, which I thought was a grim joke.

Then an encouraging letter arrived from our friends in Antwerp, holding out the hope that my parents might be able to join them.

But, as the months wore on, all communication with my parents ceased.

My father's friend in Antwerp had a heart attack and died. In addition, Zurich wrote that a letter had been returned and did I have my parents' new address.

There was now nobody left in Vienna I could write to for information. I had nightmares in which I saw my parents being transported to Poland in cattle trucks.

The call-up had reached Maurice's age group. His main concern was to complete his thesis and leave me with sufficient money for my fees at medical school (he was sure I would get in eventually), before he joined up.

"A teaching job is now out of the question, so I am going to apply for munitions work," he announced. "It pays well and I can finish my thesis and leave you in funds..."

"Oh, Maurice...!"

"There is nothing to worry about. When I was three, I am told, I took a brass fender apart and put it back together again. I threaded a Singer sewing machine at four! I also remember when I was given a toy carpenter's set of tools, but they had removed the gimlet for safety. I searched and searched for it in vain and consequently never played with the set. I'll make an excellent fitter with my MA when I get called up!"

And this is how Maurice who, after his academic education, couldn't put a screw in straight, learned in a few weeks to file with accuracy to a thousandth of an inch.

The postman's knock always sent me flying to the door. I could hear the rat-tat-tat from every room in the house. At last a letter in Father's handwriting fluttered onto the mat. I saw a foreign stamp which was neither Polish nor German, and breathed a sigh of relief as I tore open the envelope. It was written on half a page, ripped out of a school exercise book, and was undated.

> *Dear child,*
>
> *At last I am able to write to you that we are on a boat and going the same way that Leo went.*
>
> *We started on the 27.11.39. We are in good health and trust in God to help us to reach our goal. Any post we hope to receive will be through Horowitz. Let Leo know that we are in a large crowd.*
>
> *I hope that all is well with you. We shall write to you whenever possible. Let our friend Mr Heller know too!*
>
> *That is all for now.*
> *Love and kisses and special regards to all from*
> > *your Father.*

On the back was written:

> *Dear Fanny,*
>
> *We hope now to have news from you soon. We will write whenever there is a chance. Make sure Leo's address is with either K or H because we don't know whom we will first visit.*
>
> *May the Lord grant us to be there soon.*
> *Lots of love and kisses from*
> > *your mother.*

And at the bottom of the sheet:

> *Dear Frl. Doktor,*
>
> *Do you remember the youngish-old couple whom you met at the Samovar Session? We are your parents' companions on this journey.*

Kind regards,

Lutzer.

I sank down onto the bottom stair and wept with relief and anxiety as I recalled my brother's illegal nightmare journey to Palestine.

A night in a Turkish jail, weeks in detention in Constanza, then seven hundred of them packed into a leaky cargo boat; weeks in a Cypriot camp, a fire in the engine of the next boat and finally wading ashore under the shelter of darkness to escape (after two hundred days) the watching eyes of the British soldiers.

Chapter Ten

The Frozen Danube

At the end of December, 1939, everybody had a sore throat and a cough. It was freezing cold and, when I opened the front door to our milkman, a foot-high ridge of snow fell on my red slippers.

"Never known such weather – it's them foreigners what brought it in," I heard our char tell my mother-in-law.

"My love, you've brought Viennese winters to our island!" laughed Maurice when I told him of our char's verdict.

The New Year of 1940 brought more frost and snow, food rationing, a measured dim lighting of the streets and a stream of disgruntled evacuees returning to London.

Maurice was now working at the National Time Recorder Company. He filed small stamped-out metal parts, the functions of which he never did get to find out. A fitter by day and a postgraduate student, and my private tutor in the evening.

My mother-in-law was strenuously resisting my efforts to improve her health. She insisted on eating salty dishes like kippers and soused herring, which did her oedema no good at all. She seemed to positively enjoy her poor health.

For over a month I received no further letters from my parents, and then one arrived stamped from Kladovo in Yugoslavia, dated the 5th January. It had taken ten days to arrive.

Dear Fanny,

We have been sending you letters by various routes and hope you have received them. As you know we left by boat the same way as Leo, and now we are stuck here with about a thousand people. We are told the Danube is impassable, but we just don't know the real reason.

In any case, it is assumed that we will stay here for about three months. We are living on three barges in the middle of the stream. I don't mind the food, but it isn't very good for Mother. The sleeping conditions are beyond description.

To put it bluntly, we are a thousand Jewish waifs stuck in the water. But, thank God, we are in fair health. May the Almighty grant that one day we will all be reunited. We suffered a great deal after the outbreak of war. For the outlay of DM 4,500 we were promised to reach our goal in four weeks. We were so desperate that when we were offered two bunks on the boat we were happy to accept, and were indeed overjoyed. Of course, it never occurred to us that it would take all this time!

We are told that we won't now get away until March or April. Who knows what may happen before then?

You can imagine how things stood with the Jews in Vienna, that I resorted to this journey. It was a difficult decision – a matter of life or death.

Now, please write in detail how you are. Let us know Leo's address. Did he get his trunk in the end? Also, let us have Karl's and Sali's addresses.

Lots of love from your

Father.

In the remaining space Mama wrote:

Dear child,

It is more than two months since we last heard from you. You can't imagine what joy a letter from you is for us! I can tell you one thing: I sleep much better here in our bunk than I did in bed in the Komoedianten Gasse in Vienna. Even healthwise, I feel better.

Kisses and much love from your

Mother.

The address I was given was c/o Mr Spitzer in Belgrade (the brother-in-law of Mrs Lutzer). Now, at least, I could write to my parents and was able to tell them that I had got married and was very

68

happy. I enclosed some snapshots of Maurice and myself, the garden and our rooms.

I awaited their response with some apprehension.

One week later a heavy envelope dropped onto the doormat. Three letters directed to various addresses in England and two large sheets from my parents fell out.

Dear Children,

Heartfelt congratulations! We wish you happiness and God's blessings in all you undertake. May the Almighty bring peace and enable us to join you. Your letter has both surprised us and overjoyed us. The whole boatload shared our excitement and congratulated us. We cried and laughed as we handed your pictures around.

We were in despair in Vienna during the last few months, and that is why we decided to join such a hazardous journey, trusting in the Lord to help us to unite once more with our children. Even though it was not granted to us to witness your wedding, we hope to join you one day! There is eternal hope in the Jewish breast.

Dear Maurice, forgive us for not being able to answer your dear letter. It arrived on the day of the outbreak of the war and we were in dire distress – words fail me to describe it. We have to thank God to have escaped with our lives.

Now, my dear Children, we are on the river – think of us and wish us luck! Try to get in touch with Leo and write to us often! The Lord must surely help us!

But enough, I must leave room for Mama,
Love and kisses from your

Father.

PS Special regards to Maurice's dear parents – now our relations – and hopefully the good Lord will let us meet one day.

Please forward the three enclosed letters.

On the half page left, Mother had written:

My dear Children,

We wish you a heartfelt 'Mazel Tov'! Your letters have given us great joy.

Dear Fanny, may you remember your journey to London for the rest of your life as the luckiest step you have taken!

Yes, God's ways are marvellous. With God's help may you rejoice in each other. It cannot be otherwise as this alone speaks for your Maurice that he recognised his soulmate in you among so many he met in the Shelter.

Now we are worrying about Leo. I must close now to catch the post.

Love and kisses,

> *your Mother.*

Special regards to Maurice's parents.

We read and re-read the letter in front of a roaring fire in our sitting room, toasting crumpets on a long fork. My father-in-law had laid in a large stock of coal during the summer and our Victorian fireplace swallowed chunks the size of watermelons like hazelnuts.

Outside, the whiteness of the snow was blinding. Shrubs and trees blended into an arabesque, seen through the frozen window panes.

I felt unworthy of my good fortune. In spite of their plight, my parents' main concern was for my brother and myself.

That same evening I wrote to tell them of the safe arrival of their precious letter. The next post arrived two weeks later.

22.1.40

My dear Children,

I wrote to you last Tuesday, but as I expected a reply to my letter days ago we are very worried. Please write at least one postcard and one letter every week. You can't imagine what joy your letters give us. Every day your mother has said 'still no news from our children'.

Fanny, please get in touch with Leo. We are very worried about him. If he hasn't yet received his cabin trunk, how can he bear to be still wearing the clothes in which he left Vienna in February, 1939!

According to information here, the trunk should certainly have arrived!

In fact, Leo had written to me that his trunk had arrived and had contained only one shoe. 'Don't tell our parents! The Italians are known to open such luggage destined for Palestine and strip it of its contents.'

Father's letter continued:

> Now we can understand why he wrote: 'Don't travel the way I did,' writing his letter on his knees, sitting on the floor of the Detention Camp. And everything here is difficult.
>
> Yes, Fanny, you can thank God you were spared this. As you have been so lucky, please take a special interest in him. There he is, homeless and all alone.
>
> We are as well as can be expected under the circumstances. May God help us to get away from here soon. We have some prospect of continuing our journey next month.
>
> Now, let us know how you are and what is going on in the world. We have been here for two months in the middle of the river, cut off from the outside world.
>
> You won't believe it, but we are often even cheerful here. Three weddings have taken place, and last Tuesday a baby boy was born. We must remain in good health and as strong as steel, as Leo used to write!
>
> Love and kisses from your
>
> > Father.

On the next page Mother had written:

> My dear Children,
>
> When we got your letters we were overcome with joy. We especially treasure your photos. Many times during the day I chat with them. A few lines from Maurice would give us great pleasure.
>
> The whole boat was excited as it was the first letter from London and almost everyone has relatives there. Dear Fa, I know you are worried about us, but the best way to console and give us joy is to write to us often and, please, long letters.
>
> Nothing definite is known about the continuation of our journey. I hope we won't have the delays that Leo

experienced, with the additional hardship of being confined to the boat.

I leave it to your imagination to picture what happened to us in V which could force your father to join this transport. It is the same company which once reached its goal in nine days (when Leo took two hundred) – that was our inducement.

In your next letter, please enclose a few lines to Mr and Mrs Lutzer who made it possible to send you our first letter from the ship. They met you at our 'Samovar Session' and take great interest in your welfare. There is little facility here for writing, hence the pencil..."

I tried to remember the Lutzers. The 'Samovar Sessions' on Sunday afternoons were held in our erstwhile Jewish MP's flat. He would feed us information and encouragement. They were, in addition, family friends and ardent Zionists. Their son, some years older than myself, had inspired Leo with Zionist ideas. These were crowded get-togethers and I was not sure that I could now identify the Lutzer family. Nevertheless, I would of course write them a special note.

At our work table on my own – Maurice was at work – I looked out of the window at our lawn and the trees, but saw the three barges and its cargo stuck fast in the frozen Danube. It was then that I remembered our friends in Zagreb. I had stayed twice in their hotel in Crikveniza; their son had visited us in Vienna and we had remained in touch until Hitler's invasion. Perhaps they would accommodate my parents until they could continue their journey.

In my letter to my parents, after sending birthday wishes to my father, I asked whether they might leave the boat if suitable accommodation could be found. The reply came within a week.

Dear Fanny,

Your dear letter arrived yesterday just in time for my birthday and it is the best present I have ever received. We enjoyed it very much, and your mother for once couldn't sigh, 'No post from our children.'

We had a double celebration as a baby girl, born last week, was given her name and the company sang 'Happy

*Birthday' for me, and one lady even kissed me! All this
and your letter made my day a really happy one.*

*To answer your questions about leaving the boat – we
would love to and I have again spoken to our man in
charge and he told me of the difficulties: the Yugoslavs
won't allow us off the boats and the winter harbour. We
are sixty km from the railway station. We don't know
what to do. We paid our DM 4500 and trusted in God,
and now we are here and cut off from the world. We are
helpless.*

*Heller has sent me 450 Dinar, I am therefore all right
for cash. If we could only get on with our journey! May
the Lord have mercy on us – we have been nearly three
months now on these barges. I don't mind the food, but
it's not so easy for Mama, and our sleeping arrangements
are beyond description.*

*I wrote last week to Leo via Horowitz, but still not a
line from him! Why does Maurice not write more often?
I have greetings for you from Mrs Mandl and her two
daughters, and Mr and Mrs Kreliner and many more of
our Viennese acquaintances.*

*Now, my dear children, write often – that is our
greatest consolation!*

*The winter here is mild and we have heating. How
are you and Maurice? Write more about yourselves. We
hope that God will bring us together, and that keeps us on
our feet!*
Love and kisses,

from your Father.

I had now established a postal routine: I despatched a postcard on
the same day my parents' letter arrived, and followed it up by a letter
during the week. Post, when regular, took ten days one way! Letters
were often read by the censor in this country, but my parents told us
nothing was ever blotted out.

One evening towards the end of March, I re-read with Maurice the
letters that had arrived that morning.

"I don't understand it," I said to Maurice. "Why don't they move
on!"

Kladova, 14.3.40

Dear Children,

Your letter of the 5th reached us today. Do go on writing regularly, please – as often as you can! This is our only joy and hope of a 'Wiedersehen'. Nothing positive is known about our outward journey.

We have received a postcard from Leo, but he doesn't say if he is working or has at last received his cabin trunk. He has given us a new address: Gruenberg in Rechovot – and we have answered him immediately. As for our progress, it is exactly like Leo's – we are stuck fast.

How are you? We are, thank God, in good health. It is amazing what one can get used to. Even Mama is sleeping better. Thank God, the winter was mild and now we are sitting on the deck in the sunshine writing to you. It's nearly four months that we have been on the boat. We are supposed to resume our journey in a few days.

Now I had better leave room for Mama, she always complains that I don't leave her sufficient space in our letters.

My dearest Children,

Every letter is a joyful event here and means hope and mental food for everyone.

For the last few days we have had brilliant summer weather and hence more sunshine in our hearts. We now stay all day on deck. I am taking part in a Hebrew course – we have one for beginners and one for advanced students. Mrs K has sent us greetings and congratulations on your marriage. She is still marooned in Vienna and is thinking of going on a similar transport!

Dear Children, don't let our circumstances mar your own happiness! In this life you must enjoy every happy moment and not allow the present to be made miserable because of an uncertain future!

Our position too is made more difficult because of the war! But we have already survived so much that we hope to get through this too and tell you one happy day about it.

Leo writes nothing about himself. I am worried about his unsettled way of life. It is lovely to sit in the sun and I feel really well. There is a lot of talk of progressing with the journey, but I am sceptical. Still, let us hope! I love you very much,

Mother.

"In all their misery," I said to Maurice, "Mother thinks of our happiness and is concerned not to spoil it."

"If only we could do more for them!" he sighed.

"Perhaps our friends in Zagreb can help," I murmured.

The reply came from Zagreb a few days later, dashing that last hope. They wrote that my letter had just reached them as they were packing up to leave for South America. It arrived in the same post as another from my parents in which they stated that none of them were allowed to leave the boat and go on land; and then, almost as if to cheer me up:

Here among the thousand of us we are a very mixed bunch. We have actors, musicians, an opera singer, and they have composed a revue – a tragi-comic piece about our transport. Thus the days are passable, but our sleeping arrangements! Still, thank God, we are well and in fact I sleep better here than in Vienna. If only we could reach our goal soon.

In addition to my concern about my parents, now came the ever increasing call-ups and my growing pile of rejections for a job.

Chapter Eleven

Bertha

As if to compensate us for the harsh winter, the first days of spring were sunny. By the end of March the Japanese cherry trees were in bloom and, walking down the drive one Sunday, we noticed that the candles on the chestnuts in front of the house were about to flower.

We had been discussing Chamberlain's reassurance that time was on our side and that the economic blockade would bring Herr Hitler to his knees. Maurice was doubtful, but I was in an optimistic mood. We had decided to treat ourselves to a lunch at Lyons Corner House, where for one shilling and threepence you got a three course meal and a three band concert of classical continental favourites thrown in.

Apart from rationing and the busy removal of iron railings, the war seemed to be in suspended animation. I was occupied with housework, typing, endless letter writing and practising Gregg's shorthand.

St. James' Park, with its subtly disguised diminutiveness, was my favourite spot for relaxation.

Occasionally, we took a boat out on the Serpentine in Hyde Park. While Maurice rowed, I leaned back against the cushions and day-dreamed of peace, with my parents restored to safety, Maurice at my side and Europe free once more.

It was on one such Sunday of the 'phoney war' that we strolled in the warm sunshine along the lakeside, licking our tuppenny Walls' choc-ices and watching the people feeding the ducks.

"Oh, look!" Maurice suddenly exclaimed. "There are Philip and Bertha!"

We stopped in front of a couple. The man was in khaki uniform and she in a flowered silk dress. Maurice introduced me. They had got married since Maurice had last seen them.

Philip was slim, not much over five foot two and his light brown hair was neatly tucked under his soldier's cap. Bertha, an inch or so taller, wore her coppery red hair swept up over her high forehead.

Phil was an old school friend of Maurice's, but they hadn't met for some time.

The men immediately started to discuss old school friends, so Bertha took my arm and we walked ahead.

"We had heard that Mo – that's what we always called him – had married a 'foreigner'," she said, smiling. "How exciting! Do tell me all about yourself." And, to encourage me I presume, she told me about her work. She had a BSc in chemistry, gained in evening classes while working to earn the fees. She was now wasting her time testing thermometers.

From this chance meeting sprang a friendship which lasted for the next forty odd years – in fact, to the end of Bertha's life. She remained in the capital all through the war. We were soon to travel all over the country, but whenever we came to London we met up or stayed with her.

Phil was working in the War Office in London; later he transferred to the Orkneys. There came years when, in spite of our correspondence, we lost touch. But when we met up again we took up where we had left off.

When Phil was called up, Bertha had set up home for her brother and her younger sister, Becky, both at college. Her parents had evacuated to Bedford.

In the following years I often stayed with Bertha. We chose Becky's first evening dress together. By pooling all our coupons we managed to obtain a sky-blue organdie dress and dancing shoes. The dress had a high neck and short puffed sleeves which went over a darker blue satin underslip. Her straight, dark brown hair we curled mercilessly with tight rollers overnight. Thus we turned a tomboy with dirty fingernails into a young 'debutante'. Her boyfriend could hardly believe his eyes when he came to call for her the next evening.

Chapter Twelve

Sunshine and New Hope

Every morning I tried to pretend that I was not listening for the postman's knock. I dusted my dressing table, polished the mirror and picked up the button I had carefully preserved to sew on Maurice's shirt. But at the first knock on the door I dropped needle, cotton and button and ran downstairs. Dashing into our sitting room, I sank onto the settee and read:

Dear children,

We have just received your letters postmarked the 8th and 26th, which gave us great joy – especially the first one which contained Maurice's addition.

We are told that we will soon be on our way. We wait. It is a bit like Leo's ordeal. Hopefully we will reach our goal.

What about the crate with our furniture? Shall we ever see any of it again? In spite of all your mother's and my work, our entire belongings have apparently been lost.

Uncle Karl gave us very misleading advice when he told us to take everything slowly. We have wasted precious time. And Leo's cabin trunk! Has the poor boy received it at last?

We were left unmolested in our own flat at first which lulled us into a false feeling of 'things being not as bad as all that'. Now I understand that when Leo wrote that Constanza would be imprinted on his mind to the end of time. I too will remember the 'here and now'.

But we must trust in the Lord – you were destined to go to London, which you resisted as long as possible, and

*found your happiness; and for us, alas, it was this. I
think it is high time for our luck to change.*

*Forgive me for pouring my heart out to you, but
sometimes it is overflowing.*

*Well, rumour has it that we will soon be on our way,
so address further letters to us c/o Jewish Community
Centre, Belgrade, Box No. 599 (KL).*
With love and kisses,

from your Father.

My dearest Children,
*Today's letter is rather sombre, but we must hope for the
best! The times are serious for all of us.*

*Regarding your enquiry as to what to send us, I think
it is too late. We are supposed to be on our way next
week. Alas, by now we receive such announcements with
scepticism. Parcels up to 40 kg are duty free.*

*Hopefully, our next letter will be en route. I am
grateful that we are OK healthwise.*
Love and kisses,

your Mother.

I was furious with myself for not enquiring earlier about sending
parcels. I collected my ration-book and took the bus to Whitechapel. I
bought mainly tins of kosher sausages, fish and biscuits. Finding a
box, I made up a neat parcel, filled in some postal forms and sent it on
its way.

I don't think my parents ever received it.

Maurice had left early for the 'Time Recorder' factory near London
Bridge and I was alone waiting for the second post. I filled in the time
with washing up the breakfast dishes, tidying our room and finally
writing out a shopping list for the weekend.

It was rather a special weekend – my first birthday in England. I
had decided that we should have Wienerschnitzel and potato salad. I
hoped to persuade our kosher butcher to let me have the right cut for it.
Besides, it was the only dish I really knew how to prepare! We would
have a real Friday dinner: candles and a glass of my father-in-law's
excellent home-brewed red wine which reminded me of our Tokay at
home.

Then there came a rat-a-tat and I dashed to the door. Impatiently, I tore the envelope open. Skimming the first paragraph, I read:

Regarding the continuation of our journey, we are now told that it's purely a matter of finance! God knows how long we will remain marooned on the water. This week we were joined by another group and now – incredibly – there are 1200 of us!

What can we do? It must be God's will! But we haven't lost hope. God has helped us to survive the winter. He will continue to help us.

We are, thank God, in fair health and your mother is diligently learning modern Hebrew! She is at this very moment translating something as we both sit at the table. The course consists of eight students and she is top of the class. I am afraid I am too impatient for such pastimes.

When the weather is fair we sit out on the grass and the youngsters go in for games. Thus the days pass. It's the nights I dread! Luckily the nights are shorter now.

Now, dear Fanny, I congratulate you on your birthday! I wish you health and happiness with your husband. May God grant us to celebrate your next one with you.

On Sunday the 14.4 at 8.30 p.m. we shall drink to your health and prosperity and you, too, must drink a glass of wine at that time so that we are united in spirit across the Great Divide! Don't despair, I am hopeful that we shall all unite one day.

How about Maurice? Write in detail.

Love and kisses,

Father.

Mother's letter started with '*My dear Fannerle*'; she hadn't called me that since I was a small child and grazed my knee in a fall. I felt her warm embrace.

First my heartfelt best wishes for your birthday! May God grant you to celebrate all your future birthdays in joyous unity with your Maurice. May we be granted to join you!

Leo worries me very much! We also worry about Maurice's call-up. Nevertheless, chin up and don't lose hope. Papa exaggerates about my Hebrew, but it is a pleasant diversion for me from the everlasting lamentations.

Thank God, our health is standing up to it and that's why I feel everything will come out right in the end.

Lots of love to both of you

from your Mother.

Regards to M.'s parents.

'Dear Mama and Papa!' I sighed; 'in all their distress to remember the exact time of my birth! Yes, we will drink to your safely reaching your goal and a future birthday together!'

How thoughtless of me to mention my concern about Maurice's impending call-up. I got up and went into our room to write an immediate reply. I reassured them about Leo. I told them that he had in fact sent back my international stamps which I included in all letters, stating "I am earning my living. I can afford to buy stamps. Stop worrying about me." Then I went on to describe some of the work I was doing.

At that time I was typing the first draft of Maurice's thesis and spending most days at home. I answered every advertisement I could find for work as a laboratory assistant in hospitals, and included English translations of the glowing testimonials I had earned for six months' work in Vienna.

I tried Guy's in London and St. Margaret's Hospital in Essex – and in despair even wrote to the Victoria Hospital in Blackpool – but was never even called for an interview. Only polite letters of rejection arrived, which of course I didn't mention to my parents.

I went on with my domestic work and tried to improve my cooking skills. Maurice bought me Harben's cookery book, geared to our rationing, and I also tried to imitate dishes we had both liked in restaurants.

Towards the end of April, my father wrote:

Our position is now as follows; we were told that as soon as the Danube becomes navigable we will go on. This is how we were consoled. At last we have now been told that it is a financial matter and that whoever has an immigration permit can leave. None of us, of course, has one.

Now we are allowed to leave the boats, I have little hope of continuing our journey. We are to be housed in a hutted camp and considered as Yugoslav immigrants. We may be able to live privately if we leave the party. We may get a small amount of financial support like other immigrants before us. We are now all beggars.

I don't know what to do. Health-wise it would be better for Mama to live privately. For four months now we haven't slept in a bed. It is amazing that we stayed well.

Here we have fresh air, how it will be in a camp I don't know.

Why has everything I have undertaken gone wrong? I must assume this is God's will. We were reluctant to go on this kind of transport but there was finally no other way out.

In all this horror our only consolation is your happiness. Please write every week. This is our lifeline. We know you too have worries. Let us know and perhaps we can advise you and you can advise us.

My whole fortune and possessions are lost, but I no longer care if only the Almighty might help us to unite again.

If you can, send me two or three pounds in a registered letter (not by postal order). It's not terribly urgent. I can help myself.

We wish you a happy Passover.

It was the bottom of the page and no room for Mama. I also knew that the money must be very urgent or Papa would have never asked for it. We despatched five single pound notes with a short English letter to avoid the delay of the censor.

The dissatisfaction with Chamberlain's leadership had grown after Hitler invaded Denmark and Norway in short succession, and Churchill was called on to lead the country. He formed the 'National

Government' and created the Home Guard. He appeared to inspire the nation.

In our family there was rejoicing over my sister-in-law's first baby boy.

During the first week in May, Leo too wrote a hopeful letter saying that he had met an old friend of our parents who had promised to pull strings to get father a businessman's visa into Palestine. Our spirits were uplifted; the sun shone and birds sang in the garden.

One fine warm Sunday I had persuaded Maurice to have our 'brunch' in the garden. My mother-in-law had already been up for some hours and was taking a rest in her room. Maurice sat in the garden near the bird table. He had taken the day off serious work on Georg Büchner and was brushing up on Hegel – a philosopher profoundly antipathetic to Büchner.

Our black cat was cruising round him and from time to time rubbing an ear against his ankle, miaowing quietly for attention. But Maurice was quite oblivious to his surroundings.

While boiling eggs, percolating coffee and preparing open sandwiches in my Viennese style, I smiled as I remembered our last night's disagreement. Maurice had maintained that philosophy was the pillar of civilisation. I disagreed.

"What is the use of just thinking? As we were told in our 'Philosophische Propaedeutik' (the art of thinking) lessons in Vienna, it's Observation, Experimentation and Application – in short, scientific action – that led to progress and civilisation."

Maurice countered, "But it is the thinker that lays the foundation for…"

"Yes," I interrupted, "and some funny 'thinks' they come up with. That Bishop – I forget his name – 'the chair you see is there while you are there to see it and when you are not there it doesn't exist'!"

"Now you would pick on Bishop Berkeley," Maurice laughed.

"Why not? He is a philosopher." I made to leave for the kitchen. "My humble cooking needs me more than your philosophers."

"No, it doesn't," Maurice said, scooping me up in his arms and lifting me onto the enormous Victorian mantelpiece. "Now you can concentrate and the cooking can wait."

There I was, stuck up on the marble shelf five foot above the marble surround on the floor. Maurice turned to his book-case, fishing out volume after volume and placing them on our worktable.

"Now, Aristotle for instance..."

But I wasn't listening.

"And there is the Englishman, Mr Locke, with his *Essay on Human Understanding...*"

I was not going to be inveigled into discussion. How to get down was my problem, not philosophy.

"If you like we will start with Plato and..."

I stretched out my hand for the book and as he came near I got hold of his shoulders and slipped down, while Plato landed on the marble surround.

"You little...!"

But I was quicker and before he could get hold of me I had ducked under his elbow and run into the kitchen.

Alas, the outcome was charred potatoes and partly burnt meat which Maurice was eating with great gusto just as my mother-in-law, who had had her meal earlier, came in for her tea. She paused, looking on with horror and disgust. Her silence said more than any words could have done.

"I think, my love, you have discovered a new dish and it tastes delicious," Maurice laughed.

As I assembled the tray, I thought, 'Philosophy and casseroles don't mix, remember that next time.' Walking carefully down the iron steps, I was immediately greeted by our cat; he did not love me, but condescended to demand food when it suited. Maurice too put Hegel aside to eat.

Over coffee we re-read my parents' letter which had arrived with the morning post. They too appeared more hopeful:

> *Since the weather improved we have been allowed to leave the boats and sit on the nearby meadow, but we are not permitted to enter the village. Only those who leave the party can take up lodgings in the camp or live privately. But this is not definite. Those who have an entry permit to another country will be able to visit the respective Embassy in Belgrade.*
>
> *Leo writes that he has collected all the documents and affidavits and is trying hard for us.*
>
> *Yes, our journey was 'die reinste Fahrt ins Blaue', (truly a journey into the unknown). The company appears not to have been properly organised and to have relied on*

favourable chances. We knew nothing about this. A second group which left later has long since reached its goal. To think we might have joined the second party, which was cheaper too, but this one was supposed to be one hundred percent reliable! Yes, everything is Destiny! Still, I believe the Lord will assist us to unite one day and talk over our adventures in a joyful family circle.

Chapter Thirteen

Invasion Fever

The mood of elation was not to last long. Some days later as I walked down Brixton Road, a trainload of soldiers waved to us as the train crossed the bridge coming from Victoria. They were the lucky ones who had survived the Dunkirk beaches. 'The undefeated expeditionary force' we were to read in the newspapers.

Then came Churchill's rousing speech of defiance: "I can offer nothing but blood, toil, tears and sweat!"

Did anything of this reach those boats on the Danube or my brother on the kibbutz? I immediately wrote letters emphasising our undisturbed life for reassurance. Then rumours reached us that two thousand male aliens living within twenty miles of the English coast had been removed to camps. Later seventy thousand were shipped to the Isle of Man and then further afield to Canada and Australia. A fear of invasion gripped the nation and with it came the dread of a 'fifth column'.

I had become painfully aware of my Austrian accent and tried to improve my pronunciation by listening to the wireless and the acceptable diction at the time in American films. We watched films like *Gone with the Wind* and *Casablanca*. The queues for the cinemas had lengthened.

The days were now hot and thundery. We learned that fifteen hundred aliens on their way to camps in the 'Andora Star' had been torpedoed and all had perished.

My next letter must have conveyed my sadness because in his reply Father wrote:

> *Dear Children, don't despair; we have food and even sleep better. One can't escape God's Will! I never wanted to be an emigrant. We were told it would take*

*four weeks at most. We paid our DM4,500 and now we
have to take each day as it comes in this world of turmoil.
With Sali's money we hope to live privately and Mama to
do the cooking. You know how well she can manage on a
little outlay. If I can get a little financial support we
won't have to queue in the soup kitchens. That's what
really hurts!*

*On the 3rd of May we left the boat to live with a
farmer's family in the village. Mama, with her gift for
languages, can even communicate with them. Kladovo is
a small town of 3,000 inhabitants. You can't imagine the
dilapidated state of the houses. General hygiene is non-
existent. In short, no washing facilities for self or
clothes. Imagine, it is worse than 50 years ago in
Jesupol in Poland!*

I knew what he meant by that as I remembered our
visit: shared earth closets and a village pump. I read on:

*There are two communal kitchens, one kosher and one
not. We have to collect our food three times a day. We
are still told that we will be able to continue our journey,
but I no longer believe it. We are told 4,000 refugee
certificates may be issued soon. I am writing to Leo in
case it comes off.*

*Now you know our condition, but don't despair! 'We
have to be as strong as steel,' Leo wrote. We have not
given up hope of joining you one day!*
Don't worry, we are in good health.

Thus my parents tried to put heart into us. We felt helpless.

In June the Germans entered Paris.
In the face of the invasion fever, Churchill assured us that we
would fight them on the beaches, in the fields, in the streets, in the
hills... We would not go down like the others! No more holidays, a
twelve hour working day. There was a rifle range at Buckingham
Palace and the King and Queen remained in residence.
Our patriotic French lady had left us for a safer place in Cornwall.
Maurice continued with his training as a fitter during the daytime, and
his thesis on Georg Büchner in the evenings.

In the same month Mussolini took Italy into the war. A few days later a tear-stained letter arrived from Leo. All his hopes to rescue our parents had been shattered. Mussolini's action meant that no ship could pass through the Mediterranean. Leo himself was suffering from sandfly fever and the heat had sapped his strength.

I sat in my usual place at our worktable and looked out at the sun-drenched garden. The roses next door vied with each other in colours of blazing red, pink and golden yellow. Blackbirds were courting on the grass and feeding each other ripe cherries. High above the treetops our silver barrage balloon swayed on its ropes. But above it all, white trails of our Spitfires belied the apparent peace.

I tried to persuade myself that perhaps it was as well for our parents to hide out in a forsaken Yugoslav village. I went on writing letters to my uncles to explain the necessity of sending regular remittances as Father had told me that dollars had a more favourable exchange rate. In any case it was my parents' money they were holding in trust. With Leo I could commiserate, but the letters to my parents were the most difficult ones. I would sit in front of the white sheets of paper, fill my fountain pen, blot a line, start again on a new sheet and try to forget what was really on my mind.

Thus we entered July and the 'Battle of Britain'. The daytime raids were so severe that the evacuation of children was restarted. Free passage to Canada and the USA were offered. Then a shipload of seventy-three children was torpedoed; all were drowned and the evacuation was stopped.

Rumours circulated that invasion barges had been prevented from landing, and that a further ten thousand 'aliens' from Germany had been removed to camps.

There was never any hint in my parents' letters that they had any knowledge of the war.

The more beautiful the day the severer the bombing became. A clear sky was a bad omen. Shopping had to be fitted in between raids. When the siren went we were supposed to go into the shelters. One day, when it had clouded over and I was hurrying to Brixton market, a sudden loud bang made us all stop in our tracks; but a woman laughed at the next bang. "It's only thunder!" and the following downpour made us all happy. It meant no raid for a while.

I had always been a bit afraid of thunder, but from that moment on I was cured.

Thus we entered September. On the anniversary of the declaration of war, Hitler made his boast: "We are coming!" On the eve of our wedding anniversary, September 9th, we were treated to a display of fireworks. The East End docks had been set alight by the Luftwaffe. We watched from the skylight of our roof.

"This country has never been invaded since 1066, and Hitler is no Norman!" Maurice reassured me.

But during the day I was now alone with my thoughts. My mother-in-law had gone to stay with her daughter, whose house had so far escaped major damage. The flats above and below had been vacated, but I didn't want to move for fear of losing all postal contact with my family.

Blown-out windows we repaired with wood and cardboard. I cleared the rubble and returned to my typing and letter writing. After one such clearing up, I cut myself on some broken glass. I cleaned and disinfected my hand, but the next morning my right index finger was hot and throbbing.

"What is the matter with your hand?" Maurice asked.

"Oh, it's nothing, just a scratch," I smiled. But I knew better, and, after seeing Maurice off, I took the 159 bus to Trafalgar Square. I turned in the direction of the Strand and crossed over to the Charing Cross Hospital.

I entered through the double doors, inhaled the familiar hospital scent and went up to the Almoner's window. I gave my name and occupation as a medical student – 'I shall soon be one again,' I consoled myself for the little white lie, ignoring my second rejection by the Conjoint Board in Edinburgh.

I dropped half a crown into the collection tin and the kindly, grey-haired almoner wrote down my complaint and directed me down the corridor.

I joined a middle-aged woman with a bandaged forearm on a wooden bench in front of a number of white curtained-off cubicles. Behind them, subdued noises of instruments and voices were audible.

A white coat passed and I sighed, wondering whether I should ever wear one again.

"Don't be afraid, my dear," the woman next to me said. She had misinterpreted my sigh and laid a comforting hand on mine. "They're ever so nice here." She looked at my bandaged finger. "Does it hurt very much? Have you cut yourself?"

"I think I picked up a glass splinter sweeping up after last night's air raid," I replied.

"Wasn't it awful! Night after night... we've got no windows now, the roof is half off. I work at..." and she proceeded to tell me about her work at a munitions factory. As I listened I became aware of the posters pinned to the wooden supports partitioning the cubicles.

WALLS HAVE EARS
and

CARELESS TALK COSTS LIVES

And here I was, with my foreign accent, being told all about a munitions factory.

A curtain moved and an elderly woman came out.

She had a neatly bandaged head. The nurse who followed her called me. I said goodbye to my companion and entered a square cubicle with a couch. A young doctor was sitting on a stool next to it.

He read the note written by the almoner, and looked up when the nurse cut my bandage off. The nurse handed him a probe. I thought her very attractive in her stiffly starched apron and the white cap fixed like a tiara on her wavy dark hair.

"Will you be coming to the dance?" he asked her as he gently lifted a small flap of skin. He looked up at me questioningly.

"Yes, I am afraid it hurts," I said.

"Certainly, if you'll take me," the nurse answered coquettishly as she handed him an alcohol swab.

"I'm not sure when I'll finish," he remarked. He turned to me: "I shall have to enlarge the cut to look for the glass splinter. We'll give you a whiff of gas."

I agreed with his diagnosis and procedure but resented his private discussion.

Stretched out on the couch, I took some deep breaths through the mask and walked out into a Hobbema-like tunnel of green trees.

I awoke to the conclusion of their conversation. "... is bringing his record player," the nurse remarked as she bandaged my finger.

"I think this should do it. Don't hesitate to come back if it continues to hurt," said the young doctor, going to the washbasin at the back of the cubicle.

My finger healed without a scar, but I resolved never to discuss private affairs while attending to a patient.

The autumn faded and winter drew in with long dark nights. Punctually at 6 p.m. the air raid siren screamed and the German bombers thundered overhead.

I had my shopping basket ready-packed with thermos flask, sandwiches, candles and books to occupy us in the Anderson shelter at the bottom of the garden. I had sewn up blankets to form makeshift sleeping bags. We dressed in siren suits ready to dash out when incendiary bombs fell nearby. We threw dustbin lids over them to extinguish their tell-tale lights. Later on, however, they also carried explosive charges and became dangerous to approach.

I was anxious when the siren did not sound at the right time, fearing that the invasion had started on the coast instead.

A new horror was inflicted on us with the doodlebugs. They would drone overhead, then cut out, leaving us in frozen silence until the explosion on impact. In November Maurice's call-up was postponed as he had completed his fitter's training and was now engaged in war work.

Every morning at 7 a.m. he travelled to his work at the Time Recorder factory. The bus never failed to arrive, dodging the craters and rubble the night raids had invariably created.

"Hitler can't get us down!" the milkman said, holding out my bottle of milk. He departed down the drive, whistling, "I've got sixpence..."

As a Christmas present the Luftwaffe bombed the BBC.

About that time I applied to the Professor of Pathology at the Hammersmith Hospital for the post of laboratory assistant. The interview was short.

"I have experience in the preparation of tissue slides," I told him. "I worked in the Rothschild Hospital in Vienna for six months after I qualified, doing just such work."

He read the highly complimentary references in the English translation, glanced at the German original to which it was attached, and I could feel his distaste.

"We have a number of applicants to see. Thank you for coming. We'll let you know."

Within a week the letter arrived thanking me for my application, but the post had been filled.

In the same postal delivery came a letter – this time from Mother only.

My dear Children,

Thank God there is another letter from you. You can't imagine what we suffered when there was not a line from you for six weeks. We understand that letters from you go astray, so please: a letter and a postcard every week to prevent such a long interval again.

You must realise that post from our dear ones is the only spiritual sustenance, and indeed diversion, we have.

Dear Fanny, I guess from your letter that you worry. If you waste your energy you won't be any help to your dear husband or us. So, chin up! I too had a very hard time at your age in the First World War. Please, dear, keep your nerves steady if you love us.

You would be surprised to see how courageous I am, only missing news from you can get me down. You might tell your uncle Sali of our misery stuck here and penniless. Thank God Leo's letters are more hopeful. Together I am sure we could make a go of it.

Well, dear Children, don't despair.
Love and kisses,

from your Mother.

No line from Father. Was he ill, or too depressed to write?

I sat down to write immediately to my uncle. And another to my parents, which Maurice checked to make sure there was nothing in it to worry them.

The few letters from my uncle Sali always assured me that he was doing all he could, i.e. sending money regularly and blaming officialdom and the banks for delays and failures.

Chapter Fourteen
The Maisonette

One night we were woken by the persistent throbbing of a German bomber. It sounded as if he was looking for a target just above our heads.

"He is coming down on top of us," I whispered, and drew the blanket over our heads, winding my arms around Maurice; but no explosion followed. We waited for several minutes in the silence, and then slipped out of the Anderson shelter – but all was dark and unusually quiet.

"No chocolate this time," Maurice joked. He would feed me a Black Magic chocolate each time we heard an explosion – chocolates were a luxury at that time of strict rationing. A young apprentice who had attached himself to Maurice at work supplied him with a pound box every fortnight (his mother worked in a chocolate factory). His reward was two shillings and sixpence and a free French lesson during the tea break. This was the only black market activity we ever indulged in.

Next morning we were told that the German pilot had crash-landed his plane into a side street off Brixton Hill Road and given himself up to the Home Guard.

Our wartime routine continued unabated: siren, shelter, all clear and then either to bed in our room or up for work. I learned to make omelettes with dried egg powder. I had never cooked one even with fresh eggs! On occasional Saturdays and Sundays, whenever Maurice was free, we went for walks in the parks and enjoyed a three course meal at the Lyons Corner House at the Tottenham Court Road branch, for one shilling and threepence, we were also able to listen to a Hungarian-style orchestra. The musical trio wore red waistcoats and white blouse-like shirts. They played old classical lollipops and I could dream myself away into happy family gatherings for afternoon coffee and whipped cream.

A freezing New Year's Day greeted 1941. I was forever shovelling the Shelter path free of snow, and clearing glass and masonry away after the night's bombing.

There had been a particularly heavy snowfall during New Year's Eve. I wore my flannel pyjamas under my siren suit and the fur-lined coat that had luckily been despatched in the trunk weeks before I left Vienna. Two pairs of gloves and a pair of Wellington boots – far too large for my feet – which I had found in the cellar, completed my outfit.

A frozen bird had fallen from the tree above the Anderson shelter. Watched by our black cat, standing at the top of the stairs leading to the kitchen, I examined the stiff little body. There was obviously no hope of reviving it, so I dug a little grave for it and covered it with snow.

Our cat had not followed my mother-in-law when she joined her daughter. His meals he disdainfully accepted from me, but when I tried to stroke him he would bare his teeth with a furious hiss and hunch his back. Maurice, however, was always greeted with a friendly miaow and purrs of pleasure when he was picked up.

The bombing continued during January. "Give us the tools and we will finish the job!" Churchill pleaded with Roosevelt. We lost more windows, ran out of coal and chopped up furniture to keep warm.

In February there was a short lull in the bombing, but it was resumed with vigour in March. Fires illuminated the nights of blackout and even the moon seemed red.

One morning I received a letter from the Medical Board in Edinburgh announcing a third rejection. There had been no news now from my parents for months.

Then, on April 6th, the German army invaded Yugoslavia. Letters now had to be sent via my uncles in America. In the scant letters from my uncle Sali, he claimed to be sending my parents money regularly from their own funds deposited with him. Even so, he made it appear as if the money came out of his own pocket.

A few weeks later a distressed letter from Leo arrived: it told us that a dreadful calamity had befallen the passengers of the boat my parents were travelling in and we had little hope of ever seeing them again.

I refused to believe the news. I convinced myself that they were now living with a farmer's family and would be safe. As if to confirm my optimism, a telegram arrived in May, written in English: 'We are

OK send money.' This convinced me that my uncle was behaving badly, but that they were all right.

We went to the Westminster Bank, where I had deposited my first precious cheque, and Maurice pleaded with the manager. Much impressed by Maurice's excellent English, the manager promised to transfer ten pounds by some circuitous route through a branch in Switzerland. I also sent a telegram to my uncle asking him to send some money. We were never again to succeed in transferring any money.

By now the house, though still standing, had very few window panes still intact; the ceilings were crumbling and the roof leaked. I decided to go flat hunting.

On the 24th of May, I stood in the agent's office of the Dashwood Estate, with high hopes of renting a maisonette in their Hyde Farm Estate in Balham. An elderly man with receding grey hair and half-glasses rose behind his tidy desk; extending his hand in greeting, he invited me to sit down in the comfortable armchair opposite him.

"My name is Boxhall. I look after the maisonettes in Radbourne Road. I see you have decided on 73A – a very well appointed residence, I might say." I did not catch the nuance of the word 'residence'. "When would you like to move in?"

"On the 31st of this month," I replied.

"Would you like to leave a deposit so that I can reserve it for you?" He reached for a pile of small green rent-books.

"Will ten shillings be all right?" I asked weakly, opening my handbag.

"That will do nicely. A further ten shillings and sixpence will be due when you collect the keys. Your name, please," and he unscrewed the top of his fountain pen.

"Stang, S–T–A–N–G, no R."

"And your husband's initial?"

"M."

"The weekly rent of twenty shillings and sixpence is due one week in advance." He handed me the green rent-book. "There you are, Mrs Stang. You have very nice neighbours and no uniforms are allowed on *our* Estate."

"No uniforms?" I stammered in surprise.

"Why? Does Mr Stang wear a uniform?" As I hesitated, he helped me out. "Is he a postman?"

"No."

"Is he a milkman?"

"No."

"...a policeman?"

"No, but he may be called up and..."

He stopped me by waving his hand.

"That's the King's uniform, *that* is quite all right!" He smiled and rose to end the interview with this ignorant foreigner. It seemed that I had entered the hallowed ranks of the British middle-classes!

We moved in the following weekend. As Maurice unlocked the door – *our* door – he offered to carry me over the threshold, but the removal men had just driven up and I felt embarrassed. We entered the narrow corridor and took stock of our new home.

To the right was a fair-sized front room, and facing us were two doors; one led to a small bedroom and the other to a minute bathroom. At the end of the passage was the living room, with an old-fashioned fireplace with a back boiler. The agent had emphasised that this not only heated the room, but also provided hot water.

The adjoining kitchen and scullery opened on to a narrow strip of garden. It boasted a somewhat neglected lawn, with a herbaceous border and hedge roses which divided it from the neighbouring garden. All the window panes were intact and the whole estate appeared to be completely untouched by the bombing.

I was cheered when, a week later, an air-letter from one of Maurice's friends reached us, although addressed to our old home. But as time passed, there was still no word from my parents. I buried my aching concern deep down and tried to deal with each day as it came.

We could now sleep peacefully in our bed, only occasionally woken by the sound of bombing in the distance. We heated our bath water in the large, gas-heated copper in the scullery and carried it in buckets to our bath. I never lit the grand fire in the sitting room with the back-boiler after Maurice's futile attempt which filled the whole maisonette with smoke. He had used up three precious bundles of firewood, one copy of *The Times*, two *Daily Mirrors* and our whole meagre stock of firelighters.

June brought clothing rationing: 66 coupons each for the year. I learned to stain my legs with permanganate instead of wearing stockings. The more artistic and vain even drew a dark seam on the flesh.

Our pink hedge roses had opened up when on one glorious Sunday morning we heard, through the open window on our neighbour's wireless, the announcement of Hitler's invasion of Russia – in spite of his non-aggression pact. Maurice hugged me and whispered: "Good old Joe, just in time! This will surely save us."

To celebrate, we took the bus into the West End and, as we walked in a sun-drenched St. James' Park, people were smiling and we overheard one elderly man say to another, "Let them kill each other!"

"What a churlish welcome for our sorely needed ally," and Maurice ground his teeth in anger.

A hot July coloured into August. Letters of rejection followed applications for jobs as regularly as night followed day.

In desperation, I had started to apply for jobs further afield and at last a likely sounding appointment for an interview arrived – from Birmingham.

Chapter Fifteen
Lucas Ltd. Birmingham 1941

Maurice had taken the morning off to see me off at Paddington Station, and he carefully selected a window seat in a non-smoking compartment facing the engine.

"Now, remember: if you are offered the job, accept it on the spot!"

"But what about you in London?"

"You find us a place and I'll follow. There's a famous small arms factory in Birmingham. They must be desperate for workers."

"Oh, Maurice, but..."

"No buts!" he laughed. "You forget I'm now a qualified fitter, capable of filing to a thousandth of an inch."

"But your thesis..."

"I've completed the basic research. I can write it up anywhere."

The whistle blew. We were still alone in the compartment. He hugged and kissed me, and then jumped off the moving train. Running alongside the open window, he shouted: "I'll be meeting every train after 6 p.m. There are some very good bookstalls here!" He laughed, waved and was veiled in steam as the train gathered speed. Then he was gone.

I was sorry to make my first journey in England on my own. Then a previous parting flashed into my mind and my heart contracted, remembering my parents blotted out by the steam of my departing train on the platform in Vienna.

You will be required to carry out periodic blood tests on the workers in the car battery section to prevent them developing lead poisoning.

Thus ran the letter which had invited me to the interview. I had read up on 'lead poisoning' in the British Museum Reading Room and the work sounded quite interesting. With good medical care and supervision, I was sure such poisoning was preventable.

I got out Shaw's *Pygmalion*, which I had started to read some days ago. I always read Shaw prior to an interview. If only I could have discarded my accent as readily as I had the Austrian feather in my hat! However, the example of Eliza Dolittle gave me some encouragement; if she could learn to speak like an English lady, then so could I.

The train passed through a tunnel and I looked at my reflection in the window. I had brushed out my curls and arranged my hair in a neat roll, half-moon in shape. I adjusted the small white bow of my blouse and the lace handkerchief in the breast pocket of my navy blue jacket before returning to Eliza.

Dr Capel, the head of the medical department at Lucas Ltd., had his office in Great King Street. I reached his room after running a gauntlet of porters and secretaries. It was luxuriously carpeted and furnished in dark mahogany. Dr Capel, immaculately dressed in a dark lounge suit, shook hands with me.

"Please take a seat, Mrs Stang." I noted that he had omitted the 'Dr' and, as he looked down at me, I could feel myself shrinking by the second.

He sat down and opened the file in front of him. It contained my letter of application, the attested copy of my Viennese MD (in Latin!), and the two glowing German testimonials in English translation. This time I had kept the German originals in my handbag, which I clutched on my lap with both hands. He carefully read through my papers while a clock solemnly ticked away the seconds, and I prepared myself for a searching examination in haematology.

He seemed to take an age as he removed each sheet to study the next. Finally, he read through my MD document and turned it over to look at the Austrian and English Embassy stamps on the back. Nodding, he pushed it towards me.

"I see you are familiar with the examination of blood slides, but we need not go into that." I felt let down.

He then explained that I was to work at the branch factory in Fore Street. The salary was four pounds a week and my status would be that of laboratory assistant.

"Is that satisfactory?"

"Yes," I whispered.

"Can you start next week?"

Suddenly struck dumb, all I could do was to nod.

Dr Capel then lifted the telephone and asked his secretary for some numbers. I paid no attention.

"I have a job!" It was singing in my ears. "I have a job in England!" I could not wait to run to Maurice with the news, to write to my parents and to let Leo know!

Suddenly I realised that Dr Capel had stopped phoning and was speaking to me.

"... and you will work under the supervision of Dr Scott." He hesitated before adding, "You will be addressed as *Mrs* Stang." Was that to confirm my inferior position?

At that moment a liveried chauffeur arrived. Dr Capel rose, extended his hand over the table and, for the first time, almost smiled.

"Goodbye, Mrs Stang, I hope you will be happy with us. Jenkins will take you to our branch in Fore Street where Dr Scott will go into the details of your daily routine."

Outside a large car was drawn up at the door. I would have preferred to sit next to the chauffeur, but was too shy to say so. In the back seat I seemed too remote to start a conversation. I looked out into the grey street and wondered what Dr Scott would be like. Then I pulled myself up: 'I have a job in England, nothing else matters!'

It was a short and silent journey. We entered the gates of a very busy factory yard. 'Music while you work' blared out from surrounding workshops and mingled with the clash of metal being loaded into lorries.

We drew up at a one-storey building with an entrance to the surgery at one end and the laboratory at the other.

A white, half-glazed door opened onto a small, square waiting-room with half a dozen wooden chairs along two sides of the whitewashed walls. On my left another door opened onto a rectangular office. Its large window with opaque glass shed a dim light on the dark green metal desk, and a filing cabinet. But it was the large and incredibly modern microscope on the desk which immediately made me feel at home.

A tall man in a Harris tweed jacket partly covered by his white coat, came in. The earpieces of a rubber stethoscope dangled from his side pocket.

"Welcome, you must be Dr..." He hesitated as he extended his hand.

"Stang," I smiled, "and you must be Dr Scott."

"Right first time. Dr Capel showed me your documents and I was afraid you might be using your maiden name, so difficult to pronounce." He shook my hand in a firm, warm grip. "Well, let me show you around. This is your office. I am glad you have decided to join us." He pointed to the door by which he had just entered. "Come in and I'll introduce you to the virago who rules us all with a rod of iron."

The surgery was large and well-equipped with glass-fronted white steel cabinets, an examination couch, washbasins, sterilisers and a screen folded up in the far corner.

A slim, white-coated nurse, her blonde wavy hair partly covered by a small white cap, came towards us. I noted her navy blue belt and silver buckle.

"Meet Sister Lyons."

We shook hands. A nurse with a white belt, standing at the far end near an instrument trolley, was bandaging a workman's hand.

"And this is Nurse Magnall."

I noted the difference in status. She turned and we smiled at each other.

"Now, Sister, what about a cup of tea?" Dr Scott led me back through my future office into a small, simply furnished adjoining rest-room. He indicated a chair and we sat down. "Now, Dr Stang..."

I interrupted him. "Excuse me, but Dr Capel suggested that I should not be addressed as 'Doctor'."

"Ochey, did he indeed?"

Sister entered with a tray on which a teapot, cups and saucers, and a plate of digestive biscuits were neatly arranged.

"Dr Stang, in your honour we even get biscuits. Usually, I am lucky if I get the tea in a tin mug," he laughed.

"Oh, Dr Scott, you are naughty!" Sister smiled.

Over tea, we discussed the daily routine and when we were joined by Nurse Magnall she suggested putting me up until we could find suitable accommodation. I really felt that they wanted me to join them as soon as possible. I felt welcomed by the warmth of their reception.

Dr Scott gave me a lift to the station and as I rushed for the train I caught sight of a headline:

LENINGRAD SURROUNDED!

Hitler, I comforted myself, is no Napoleon; the Russians will beat him, too. The offensive will pin down more of the German forces and leave none to pursue the Jewish refugees in Yugoslavia.

I soon settled down into a routine of work and was determined to tighten up lead shop discipline. Apparently there had been a nasty case of lead poisoning in the previous year. I called a meeting of the foremen of the various workshops, where there was a potential lead hazard, and suggested a simple policy.

"I shall make unannounced visits to check that the lead workers are wearing their protective masks and clothing. At the same time I shall be looking for tell-tale bottles of milk left undrunk in the canteen. Please help me by your vigilance in this matter."

I knew that the staff were keen to avoid another case of lead-poisoning. It had to be reported to the Ministry of Health Inspectorate and inevitably brought discredit to the supervisory staff.

Most of the employees in my care were unskilled Irish labourers who did not believe in following what they saw as irksome instructions such as wearing a mask. Even drinking a pint of milk during the break was too much for them. The calcium in the milk combined with any lead absorbed, and it would be safely deposited in the bones. Safe – at least for the time being.

Soon I found myself being consulted, especially by the women, on general health matters. Any woman who might be pregnant had to come off lead work immediately. This was often much against their inclination and explanations and persuasion were needed on my part to convince them. There was a lower rate of pay for work in lead-free shops. The men had their own particular problems: heavy drinking and carelessness in matters of hygiene led to high blood levels of lead absorption, which showed up in their routine blood tests. These men also were excluded from work in the lead shops.

It amazed me just how many of the girls managed highly elaborate hairdos under their caps. One morning a charming twenty-year old with curls like spun gold presented herself for a routine test.

I began with the usual questions while I prepared the glass slide to examine under the microscope.

"Are you keeping well, Miss Hopkins?"

"Oh yes, doctor."

"Your bowels regular?" She nodded. (Constipation could be an early sign of excessive lead absorption). "When was your last period?"

"Two weeks ago, doctor."

As I carefully slid an exquisite curl aside to expose her earlobe for the puncture to extract two drops of blood, a plump golden louse crawled lazily out of the disturbed curl into another. A closer look at this golden beehive revealed more signs of life. I applied the alcoholic swab to her earlobe and wondered how I could approach the delicate subject without offending her.

"Do you sleep well?"

"Oh yes, doctor."

"How do you manage to do your hair so beautifully each morning?" I smiled at her and pressed the elastoplast dressing on her earlobe.

"Oh, I don't do it in the morning."

"You sleep...?"

"Yes, I put a net over my head before going to bed."

"And do you wash and set your hair yourself?"

"I don't wash my hair between visits to my hairdresser each month." She smiled at my ignorance.

"Isn't it itchy?"

"Yeeees, a bit."

"You know, somewhere you must have picked up an infestation and that's why it itches." She looked at me in surprise. "Talk to Sister. She has ways of getting rid of it."

At our lunch-break, Sister Lyons was more vocal on the state of Miss Hopkins' livestock.

"What a hairdo, and all alive! When I showed her one you would have thought she'd never seen such a creature!"

"I hope you won't..."

"Don't worry, I'll keep it confidential. But wait until I see Doris, her hairdresser – disgusting! I'll slip her one of our bottles. Lucas won't miss it and it's for the good of all."

But there was also a more serious incident. One morning a girl was brought into the surgery; she had almost been scalped. She had left off her regulation cap and her hair had got caught in the driving wheel of her machine. A guard which was usually in place had been removed for some mechanical reason. We could do little for her except clap a sterile dressing over her head and rush her to the hospital. Other than this sad incident, there was no serious accident during the time I worked at Lucas.

Chapter Sixteen

Judy

On the first weekend at my new job, I went back to London to assist Maurice. He was arranging his transfer to the BSA (British Small Arms) factory in Birmingham and was feverishly completing some final items for his MA thesis.

On our hall table I found an open army airmail letter from one of Maurice's friends. It had been carefully re-addressed to us by the post office. There had been no post from my parents for months now.

In the kitchen half a dozen milk bottles with various amounts of milk, and some dirty plates greeted me.

"What sort of meals have you been making for yourself?"

"Well, mostly I eat at the canteen or go to the British Restaurant. Yesterday, though, I made myself sausage and chips."

I looked up, surprised at this revelation of my husband's culinary skills. He was carefully drying a plate I had just washed.

"Mind you, they did taste funny."

"How did you cook them?"

"Well, I cut some beautiful chips, put them into the frying pan, poured some oil on top and lit the gas. Then I added the sausages."

"But you have to heat the oil first! You can't fry chips in cold oil!" I exclaimed. "They must have been inedible."

"Ah, so that's why they were so mushy. But I ate it all!" he exclaimed triumphantly.

"I think I had better find us a place in Birmingham quickly, before you develop stomach ulcers."

In November I found the 'place'. I had followed up an advertisement and arranged to meet a Mrs Austin after work. The front door of the two-storeyed house was open and I was asked to walk right in. She was peeling a potato and looked immaculate; quite out of place in front of the kitchen sink. She wore a smartly tailored green suit and seamed silk stockings, and a pair of patent leather high-heeled black pumps. No apron.

"Do you mind if I finish?" She turned a rather tired, thin face towards me. She looked every inch the efficient private secretary, which in fact she was.

At her feet lay a golden retriever, gazing up at her with questioning eyes.

"It's all right, Judy," she nodded. At this the dog came up to me, sniffed at my ankles and looked up as if to say: "I shall know you next time", before returning to Mrs Austin's side.

I was shown into the small sitting-room at the back; it had obviously been newly furnished and decorated. A highly polished round table near the window was circled by four chairs. A matching sideboard was crammed with china, while two comfortable armchairs stood on either side of the open fireplace.

Upstairs I inspected the newly-furnished bedroom.

"The double bed is also new," Mrs Austin explained. "It has never been slept in." A large dressing-table blocked the window. "The owner had the house newly furnished and then took fright when the air raids started, and evacuated to Yorkshire."

As we descended the stairs, she said: "I am afraid we will have to share the kitchen, but I don't do much cooking. We usually eat out in the evening. My husband prefers pub meals." She sighed – clearly she did not – then added with a smile, "Of course, it helps with the rations. Anyhow, I am sure we can come to some amicable arrangement."

I agreed. We had taken to each other on sight.

I moved in the following day. For three nights I regularly rolled off the convex new mattress onto the floor in my sleep, until Maurice joined me at the weekend and dented the mattress sufficiently to allow me to complete my nights in bed.

At last Maurice's transfer was arranged. During the last weekend in November I went back to London to help in the sorting of things to be taken and those to be stored. I was folding Maurice's suit in our bedroom when a letter fell out of one of his pockets. I was surprised to see my brother's handwriting on the envelope.

"Why didn't you tell me Leo had written to you?" I said. I slid out a small sheet of notepaper. The blue ink was badly blotched and the few lines hardly legible.

I don't know how to tell Fanny. I have just returned from the Wailing Wall where I have said Kaddish for our parents.

I sank down on our bed, stunned. Kaddish is the prayer for the dead.

"I don't believe it, it's not true! How can he know?"

"I think Leo has inside information from the Jewish Agency that arranged the river transport," Maurice said, putting his arm around my shoulders.

But my eyes remained dry. "I don't believe it. They are on a farm in a little village. I will write to my uncles in New York straight away."

The following week Pearl Harbour was bombed by the Japanese and five days later the Americans entered the war. Now the Germans will really have their hands full, I told myself. None of them will go searching for a few stranded Jews in a Yugoslavian hamlet.

We celebrated the first Sunday of 1942 in the Midland Hotel, Birmingham. In dim candlelight, we were served with brown Windsor soup, spam fritters with potatoes and cabbage, followed by an indefinable pudding drowned in Bird's custard. All this was eaten to the sounds of Vera Lynn singing 'Moonlight becomes you...', Marlene Dietrich's rendering of 'Lily Marlene', and Bing Crosby crooning 'I'm dreaming of a white Christmas.'.

Tramping back through the snow which illuminated the blackout, with Maurice holding my arm tightly, I felt warm and happy that we were together again. We avoided thinking how long it would last.

After the horrors of the London Blitz, the occasional air raid in Birmingham did not disturb us.

Maurice had packed and stored the furniture and all his books, except for a few essential volumes of poems and philosophy, and our faithful old 'Empire Aristocrat' typewriter. It had been pawned for £10 to buy my wedding ring and pay for our wedding breakfast. Long since redeemed, it patiently resounded to the tapping of Maurice's callused fingers and produced neat pica type for the last touches to his thesis.

For ten hours a day he worked on Bren guns. He stamped out the 'lip' of the magazine and filed off the burr. During tea and lunch breaks he read a pocket edition of Virgil secreted in his overalls.

I looked forward to our evenings together. We cleared away the dinner dishes and discussed the day's events over washing-up. Then we would settle down at the round table. One half became covered by Maurice's manuscripts, copybooks and loose typed pages. Crossed out and crumpled up sheets were smoothed out and reconsidered, or finally discarded in the old Bata shoe box which served as a waste-paper basket.

The following day I used the waste paper when Mrs Austin instructed me in firelaying.

"First you arrange the balls of paper, so. Then place your firelighters and your kindling in a pyramid with small coals on top. Light the paper, hold a newspaper in front to make it draw – and for heaven's sake, don't let the newspaper catch fire!"

She demonstrated all this, stooping in her tailor-made office suit in hazardous proximity to the black grate. Much to my surprise, I succeeded the very first time on my own.

My half of the table was covered with monographs and books on lead-poisoning. I speculated on ways of detecting the levels of lead in the circulation before the red blood cells were affected.

For hours now I had forgotten my parents and their plight. When I remembered I felt guilty; because of an irrational belief I held that by thinking of them I would keep them alive. Where had I failed them? What was happening in that Yugoslavian village under German occupation? I consoled myself that the Germans were now all at the Russian front and refused to believe my brother's sad news. Surely they couldn't spare the manpower to pursue a few penniless Jewish refugees.

Looking at the leaping flames, I listened to the murmur of Mr and Mrs Austin's voices next door and the rat-tat-tat of the typewriter. The room lay in shadow with a pool of light concentrated on the table and on Maurice's dark head. He was absorbed in his work. From time to time he would mutter, "This is no good," and the tearing of paper would break the peace. He recast the sentence, a quick review and "Yes, that'll do," followed, and tap-tap the typing resumed.

Our menage was, to all appearances, a happy one. Mr Austin worked at the local car factory as a foreman. He was what Sister Lyons called 'tall, dark and handsome'. He and his wife were a most delightful couple and both madly devoted to Judy, their lovely golden retriever. Judy had been chosen against an expert's advice. He had bluntly told them that she was the 'runt' of the litter, would have to be kept indoors when on heat and would not live long.

One evening our wartime idyll was shattered. I suddenly heard a door slam and Mrs Austin's hurrying footsteps upstairs. Judy had developed a high temperature. The lounge was converted into a sickroom and a mattress and blankets spread on the floor. Bottles and boxes of pills accumulated on the coffee table. Judy lay on her side, her chest heaving and her eyes closed. When her head was lifted she would open her eyes and look sadly at our feeble efforts to feed her medicines and pills. The vet came daily; he would examine her, survey her two hourly temperature chart and shake his head.

She became constipated because her training would not allow her to relieve herself indoors. Twice a day she had to be carried into the snow-covered garden and bedded down on newspaper. The Austins took days off in turn to look after her and sat up with her during the night. Maurice, too, took his turn of night duty, but I was excluded. I had never had a pet and was not trusted with her on my own.

On the sixth day Judy developed fits and the vet pronounced her doomed. He took her away in his van.

Mrs Austin left the blackout curtains drawn day and night. Her eyes were red with weeping. Mr Austin started to drink before breakfast. Mrs Austin recovered first and now she had a new worry.

"How long will it be before they notice his drinking at work?" she asked us.

Then one night, while drinking and smoking, he dozed off and burned a hole in one of the armchairs. She tried to mend it, but it remained only too visible. They had stopped going out together and at night we could hear his loud quarrelsome voice when he returned from the pub. It was as if a much loved child had died. Their marriage was shaken.

A month later the owner of the house gave the Austins a week's notice to leave. She had decided to return from Yorkshire.

After a dismal fortnight in a seedy boarding house shared with the Austins, we parted. We did exchange a couple of letters but then we lost touch with them.

Chapter Seventeen

On the Crossroads

We had found a new place with a Mr and Mrs Lane. He was a retired civil servant, a slim, quietly-spoken man, grey-haired and six inches shorter than his wife. He seemed to be perpetually dressed in a black suit and striped trousers, as if he had just emerged from his office in Whitehall.

Mrs Lane, only slightly younger than her husband, was truly formidable. She walked as if she had swallowed a walking stick, head high, her mottled grey hair brushed back into a chignon; her clothes from Harrods pre-war fashion. There were Draconian rules to be followed: one bath per week and the depth of water to be no more than five inches. She had marked it on the bath just a few months ahead of the government regulation to save fuel and water.

I tried to keep out of her way in the kitchen and do as little cooking as possible. This was frowned upon and construed as neglect of 'the man'. From the start it was stipulated that we took dinner together on Sundays. Our meat coupons helped to provide the joint and Mrs Lane cooked and served the meal in their dining-room. We were also expected to stay around and make conversation, listen to the news and stand to attention when 'God save the King' was played on the wireless before closing down. After that we were permitted to go to bed.

The month of March had brought cold north winds and I hurried home from the post office, having sent Maurice's thesis off to London for professional typing and binding.

I thought longingly of our open coal fire and Mrs Austin's warm welcome. On a cold evening like this she might even have lit it for me if she had reached home first. Now we had only a dwarf-sized gas fire which hiccuped hoarsely at us when lit. Dare I even light it after Mrs Lane had declared last Sunday that 'Spring is in the air'.

As I opened the door I saw a letter with an Edinburgh postmark on the hall table; the reply from the Conjoint Board to my fourth application for admission to their medical course. This time it had been accompanied by glowing recommendations from Doctors Capel and Scott. I was not going to tear it open with my heart beating a hundred to the minute. "No, I am going to prepare our meal, take a breather and then open it in a leisurely manner!" I told myself.

Shedding my coat, I hung it on the hanger allotted to me by Mrs Lane, picked up the letter and put it on the mantelpiece before laying the table.

"I don't care now. Refuse me if you like!" I thought defiantly. "It will be your loss, because I shall go straight into practice!" And with that I went into the kitchen.

In February doctors from foreign universities had been invited to apply for temporary registration. A week ago I had been accepted as Candidate 11,601.

As I peeled the potatoes and scrubbed the carrots, I contemplated the alternatives: GPs were looking for assistance because the younger doctors were being called up; hospitals must be short too, and I might even stay on and specialise in industrial medicine.

I heard Maurice's two short rings and dashed out before Mrs Lane could come out of her sitting-room.

"Get changed and washed. I'm making a Spanish omelette."

"Then indeed I must hurry!" He smiled and kissed me, then leaped up the stairs two at a time.

I was proud of my achievement in making passable omelettes with egg powder. Our ration was two boxes per month of the yellow stuff, the equivalent of two dozen eggs.

We were relaxing in our fireside chairs after the washing up when Maurice noticed the letter still on the mantelpiece.

"From Edinburgh, and you haven't yet opened it?"

"I no longer care!"

"Who are you kidding?" He laughed. "Where is the Agatha Christie?" (his name for a paper-knife).

Mrs Lane had kindly supplied us with one on the side-table. He ceremoniously lifted the steel blade and slit the envelope open. One glance at the sheet and he dropped the letter, lifted me out of the chair and kissed me.

"Congratulations, you have been invited for the pre-clinical exams in the autumn term!"

"Put me down! Let me see!"

"They must have got tired of your badgering," Maurice laughed. "You are one of the seven lucky ones this year."

For a week we continued to discuss the possible alternatives. Entering medical school again would mean two years of writing exam papers in a foreign language, paying fees out of our meagre savings, seeking cheap digs and economising on our few luxuries: the theatre, books and concerts. The other option would provide a decent income and perhaps a settled home – but only on the strength of a 'temporary registration'.

"And what happens after the war? I never want to return to Vienna. Would you want to live there?"

"England will win and will be magnanimous to those who helped her in her hour of need," Maurice assured me.

"But I shall remain a doctor with a foreign degree. I shall never feel equal!"

"You decide and I'll help you all I can with my fourteen years' experience of written exams. You'll see, correspondence courses in the subjects will give you the skill and confidence you need."

Thus my mind was made up and I started to prepare for the ordeal. At the microscope in the office, I studied histology with the slides lent me by Dr Scott and I read Boyd's *Pathology* in the evenings. I borrowed *Gone with the Wind* from the public library to unwind before going to sleep.

One night, with the end of the book in sight, I went on reading until the early hours of the morning. As I finished the massive volume it slid out of my tired hand and hit the floor with a mighty bang. Maurice stirred but did not wake. Then I remembered that Mr and Mrs Lane slept in the room below us. I heard footsteps pass our door and, half asleep, I thought, 'I must apologise tomorrow.'

Next morning we saw two sleepy figures in their dressing gowns coming up the garden path from the air raid shelter. A large hatbox dangled from Mrs Lane's right hand. I heard them ask Maurice, "Did you hear the bomb last night? And no warning either!"

I lay low in our bedroom and tried to slip out without being seen, but I was caught at the bottom of the stairs.

"Your husband says that neither of you heard the bomb last night."

"Was there a bomb?" I asked, trying to sound very innocent. I hated myself for the deception. I looked at the hatbox on the hall table feeling puzzled.

"I had to rescue my new hat!" She patted the box. I returned the 'bomb' to the library. As nobody else in the street had heard it, the bomb remained an enigma to the Lanes.

In spite of my concern for the forthcoming exams, I became more determined than ever to maintain a high standard of hygiene among my lead workers. "There will be *no* cases of lead poisoning while I am in charge," was my unwritten motto.

A Mr Murphy, however, had other ideas. He was a hulk of a man and always grumbled when he had to come for his blood tests.

"That man takes three times as long to return to his workbench as the other workers," his foreman would complain.

"All this hullabaloo," Mr Murphy would complain as he flopped into the chair. "If my turn comes, I won't kick up a fuss!"

"This is nonsense, Mr Murphy. If you wear your mask and drink your bottle of milk, you will never get lead poisoning. If you are absorbing too much lead, these tests will show it up long before you suffer any harm."

He would continue to mumble his protests while I cleaned his unwashed earlobe to take two drops of blood for the test.

"Just look at your teeth!" I exclaimed in horror as he opened his mouth to make further complaints.

"They don't bother *me*!"

"You should really see a dentist."

"So he can pull them all out?"

"I am sure some can be saved. At least see the dentist and find out!" I made similar pleas at every test session. I tried cajoling and then warning him that his rotting teeth would eventually affect his digestion.

"Don't you worry," he laughed, "my digestion is fine – and my bowels move nicely," he added, forestalling my next question. Thus we pattered on; he with his rotting teeth and I with my gratuitous advice. His health, however, remained unshakeable.

Then one day Mr Murphy reported sick. His GP's notification read 'lead poisoning'. This diagnosis was based on the appearance of a 'blue line' on Mr Murphy's gums. He also complained of colic.

Dr Aldridge of the Ministry of Health, to whom these cases had to be reported, sent a reprimand that

> ...*because of this man's bad teeth, neither the doctor nor the dentist should have accepted him for work with lead.*

I dug out a monograph by Professor Lane, an acknowledged expert on the subject, and the reference books by Aub and Fairhall. I found, as I had thought, that the blue line in the presence of carious teeth was likely to be the result of a combination of the gases produced by tooth decay and lead fumes. Bad teeth alone could not make a worker more liable to contract lead poisoning. Furthermore, lead colic was invariably accompanied by obstinate constipation.

I was furious with Mr Murphy for spoiling my record by his negligence in not wearing his mask. I found myself obliged to write reports which sided with his employers. I had always considered my role as one in which I protected the workers.

"He's swinging the lead for the last time," said his foreman, enjoying the pun. "I'm glad to see the back of him."

Both Dr Capel and Dr Scott agreed with him. The matter was settled with a golden handshake and dismissal.

For the next five months we submitted to the dictates of Mrs Lane's rules and restrictions with only minor arguments. I had come to realise that she disapproved of professional women in general, and of *me* in particular. Mr Lane tried to make up for his wife's rigidity with an exaggerated politeness.

Just like my mother-in-law, she too was convinced that Maurice was not being looked after as befitted the 'man' of the house. Mrs Lane's chance came on Sundays.

"A second helping, Mr Stang?" And with a triumphant smile and a significant glance at me she would ladle more rice pudding on to his plate. I detested rice pudding and never did find out if Maurice really liked it or only ate it to tease me.

The final nail in the coffin of my relationship with her came from a totally unexpected direction. I slipped outside my office and grazed my left forearm. Sister Lyons cleaned up the abrasion and painted it lavishly with gentian violet. When it was my turn to have a bath the following evening, I carefully lowered myself into the tub with my arm held high out of the water. But, after soaping myself, there was a huge flop. My arm touched the water and I found myself sitting in a basin of blue dye. I immediately pulled the plug out and tried to clean off the dye. Until then I had not noticed that it was an iron bath painted white. Now it had become a brilliant blue up to the government-approved five inch line. No soap or Vim, or indeed any power in the world, could remove the potent dye.

I went downstairs and humbly apologised. I explained about the accident and offered to have the bath repainted, but she said nothing.

Next morning a somewhat embarrassed Mr Lane buttonholed Maurice in the hall and told him that Mrs Lane now needed our rooms; her nephew was on leave from the army and was coming to stay.

"Can you please move out at the end of next week?"

Part Three

Chapter Eighteen

Camp Follower

Mrs Lane's notice to quit coincided with Maurice receiving his final call-up papers. He was ordered to present himself for preliminary training in Derby on 17th September, 1942. I gave notice at Lucas's in order to follow him and to concentrate on my forthcoming exams. Dr Scott kindly added his microscope to his battery of histology slides, saying, "Both will bring you luck. They saw me and my sister through our exams." I was to return them to his sister, who was then working at the General Hospital in Edinburgh.

Microscope in one hand, our typewriter under my arm and a suitcase in the other hand, I set out on my *Wanderjahre* – first stop Derby.

Maurice immediately found me a room in the home of a very friendly Jewish family. It was not far from his camp and any time he could get away we spent together. As long as he returned by a given hour all was well, but illegal absence incurred heavy penalties, for he could be charged on two counts: breaking out of camp and breaking back in again. He was never caught. On one occasion he left his gaiters in my room – I used to blanco his equipment and even polish his brass buttons to a glorious shine. A story went round that a store of vinegar was kept on hand, to be used in the event of an invasion to dull the brass. Happily the need never arose.

I usually accompanied Maurice on his way back to the camp, which was in a beautiful park in the 'natural' English style. The first officer I saw him salute was a sinister skeletal figure in a black cape. His limbs seemed to be wired to his trunk and his narrow head rested on a high collar of plaster of Paris. His rigid neck forced him to twist his whole body when he returned the salute. It was then I also noticed an empty left sleeve.

"My God, how can they...?"

"He is a Black Watch major, wounded in the last war. He's a first class trainer and the recruits like him very much," Maurice reassured me.

I wondered how they could expose raw recruits to this sacrificial monument of the horrors of war. I was haunted by nightmares of this vision and images remembered from Holbein's *Totentanz*. His gruesome *Dance of Death* invaded my cramped room.

I usually ate with the family, which was made up of a married daughter and her parents. Sheila (the Anglicised form of the Hebrew 'Shoshana' meaning lily) worked in the Rolls Royce factory and her father was a warden in the ARP. He kept his steel helmet and gas mask at the ready on the dining room sideboard. Sheila's husband was in the air force. She thought my work much harder than her own in the office and devoted some of her time to cheering me up.

"You spend too much time bent over that microscope." (It was set up on a small table in my room.) "The next evening your husband is free, you must both come with me to the local pub," she insisted.

"What does one do there?"

"You just enjoy yourself. Don't tell me you've never been to a pub!" I shook my head. "Well, I never! Your hubby has neglected your education. You'll like it. There is always a lovely atmosphere. There's a piano, and we sing and drink – in moderation, of course," and she winked. She lit a cigarette and we chatted for a while until my conscience made me excuse myself, although I was warmed by her caring thoughts for us.

"It's a date!" was her parting shot and I returned to my studies.

Maurice laughed at the suggestion. "Why not? You'll see how *we* English can enjoy life. It'll educate you in the gentle feminine art of sipping gin!"

True to her promise, Sheila took us to The King's Head in the market place. She boldly pushed open the massive door marked 'Saloon Bar' and made for a table in the corner of the crowded, smoke-filled room. Maurice collected two pints of 'Best Bitter' for Sheila and himself (it turned out that she disliked spirits after all), and a shandy for me.

Looking around, I thought it curious that most male customers seemed to prefer standing at the bar with the drinks, leaving the massive chairs unoccupied. A low, glass partition separated us from the public bar. There, at an out of tune, upright piano, a plump middle-aged lady accompanied her own raucous, but not unrhythmical rendition of 'Some Sunny Day', at the end of which she refreshed herself with several sips from the pint glass of beer on top of the piano. 'Bless Them All' (in an unexpurgated version which had to be translated for me) and 'The White Cliffs of Dover' followed without a pause. The crowd around her joined in the songs with ribald gusto. A full tankard was provided for the pianist as soon as her glass was empty. 'Deep in the Heart of Texas' came next, accompanied by clapping and stamping of feet to such a degree that I thought the floor would give way.

"So, this is a pub!" I had added to my knowledge of my adopted country.

After six weeks in Derby, the army in their wisdom transferred Maurice to a REME unit in Melton Mowbray for a six months course in repairing rifles and Sten guns.

He slept with his colleagues in the stables of one of the Royal hunting lodges. They were usually very Spartan places. One huge house could boast of only a single bathroom. Another feature of the town was a scattering of Royal cast-offs. Maurice pointed one out to me at the railway station. Her face was painted an inch thick and she was flirting grotesquely with a Canadian soldier young enough to be her son.

Maurice immediately found me a room and I settled in with the family. Mrs Bolton was a plump little woman with a warm smile. After clearing the tea things in the evening she would bathe her four-year-old daughter in the sink. It was a touching sight to see the pink little body wriggle under her mother's soapy flannel. She babbled and squealed with delight until finally, when lifted out and wrapped in a towel, she said, "Goodnight," and both mother and daughter disappeared upstairs.

Mr Bolton worked on the railways and occasionally did shift work. When at home during the day, he practised the trombone. Thus he often tantalised my ears when he worked over a passage and hit the wrong note again and again.

It was, however, a friendly home. After breakfast, Mrs Bolton would light a fire in my room so that I could study in comfort.

On 2nd of November, 1942, Maurice heard, on the evening news, of Rommel's retreat in North Africa.

"This calls for a celebration!" he cried. When he came off duty the next evening, he took me to the luxurious 'Anne of Cleves' café. Rationing appeared to have passed the establishment by. Butter, eggs and, above all, the most delicious cream cakes were served. The place was patronised by aristocratic land-girls in tailor-made riding outfits. They had alluring red lips and lacquered fingernails. They appeared to enjoy their flirtations with the soldiers of all ranks, who frequented the café whenever they were able to.

"What do the girls do?" I asked in a whisper.

"They look after the horses," Maurice informed me.

'As part of the war effort?' I wondered.

However, after a fortnight Maurice had to pack me off to Edinburgh for a practical course in dispensing and to familiarise myself with the pathological organ specimens which would be presented to me in the forthcoming exam.

I had no difficulty in finding a room from the list provided by the college. Happily, it was within walking distance of the university and the hospital. Mrs Nelson ran a small guest house in her first floor flat at 1 Warrender Park Crescent.

On the first morning I was introduced to some half a dozen Polish students, some of them already in cadet officers' uniforms. They had their own medical school. At breakfast, we were served with a large bowl of thick, hot porridge. I reached for some sugar, but was told by Mrs Nelson, "Don't spoil it with sugar, just pop some salt on it." I obeyed, but I still preferred the southern sweetening and made for the sugar bowl when unobserved. The oatmeal was followed by a four inch square and one inch thick omelette made of powdered egg, and thick slices of toast. Strong tea in very large teapots was passed down the table, often accompanied by the students' doleful complaints at the absence of any coffee. But, apart from this, meals were very much richer in meat and luxuries like cream or cake than in London.

Thus nicely fed, I made my way to Surgeon's Hall. There I met Dr Orr, the Dean, who also ran the course in dispensing. I was charmed by his friendly and helpful attitude. He advised me to consult his senior registrar regarding pathological organs.

I had approached the pathologist in Birmingham, but he had demanded an hourly fee far beyond my means. Hence my present trepidation.

"You can give me a hand," the registrar said, to my astonishment. "I've been preparing some new specimens and you can do the blurb on the labels. Just describe the significant pathological signs leading to the diagnosis." I was delighted.

Maurice must be allowed to participate in my joy and so, in my daily letter, I wrote:

> *Edinburgh is wonderful. My room overlooks the park and this morning I watched parents and children in their best Sunday hats and coats walking to church and leaving neat little black prints in the thin layer of new snow.*
>
> *Tomorrow I start work in my pathology department.*

Then I became absorbed in my work, but when I returned to my room the next day, I had to tell Maurice:

> *Darling, you have never been in a museum of a pathology department. It is like any other museum with glass bottles on shelves. They contain diseased organs. At lectures they are displayed to illustrate the disease being discussed. Each carries a note: 1) the course of the illness and 2) a description.*
>
> *This is what I do now, here is an example –*

and I drew a sketch

> *'Miliary tubercles can be seen in both lungs, with heavy involvement of the bronchial glands. A primary focus is present in the lower lobe in the upper lateral corner. The pleura appears dull and opaque.' See? It is made very easy to study it here. We never had it all laid out like this in Vienna. You had to find it all out by yourself.*

For good measure, I gave other examples I had written up that day.

Poor Maurice was horrified. *'... to think'* as he put it *'that my dainty little wife indulges in such morbid things.'*

In my next letter I tried to explain:

> *Now, darling, about your problem of horror about the connection of 'organs and the unfortunate dead' – it never troubles me. Funny, I am not such a brute, am I? I would, with pleasure, get up from a lovely meal and do a post-mortem right away. I think it is marvellous for the*

dead to be able to contribute to our knowledge and perhaps save a life through better diagnosis in the future.

Next morning a letter from Maurice announced:

London University has, in its kindness, conferred an MA degree on me!

I wrote back at once:

Please come and let us celebrate it here over the Christmas holidays. Everybody will be away. Mrs Nelson tells me she will make us special meals to enjoy!

Alas, for some reason, soldiers were stopped from travelling during the holidays.

Thus I was left with Mrs Nelson in the company of Boyd's *Pathology* and Hale-White's *Materia Medica*. Mrs Nelson indulged in cooking and fed me four meals a day. Between spells of indigestive stupor, I re-read my text books and talked to Maurice in mournful letters about my longing for him.

I am walking around, my body an empty shell without a soul, without you at my side.

In a fit of utter loneliness, I even penned a shockingly bad poem for him. But it included a reference to a hopeful future.

The written exams in pathology and *Materia Medica* worried me most. In Vienna I had had only oral exams, apart from writing prescriptions. In addition, my work in the pathology department had brought me in contact with lecturers, and they expected me to waltz through it all. I was not allowed the usual commiserations. I also felt I would be letting down my refugee colleagues if I didn't pass with credit.

I entered the examination hall shivering – and not only from the cold. It was the first week of January, 1943. The hall was laid out with individual tables – just like for 'Matura', the final exam at the grammar school in Vienna.

At 6 p.m. I was back and writing to Maurice:

Darling,

I am afraid I put you to shame. The questions were easy in pathology and Materia Medica, *but I fear I failed.*

It was terribly cold in the hall and the students took out books and copied, which irritated me immensely. I knew the answers to the questions, but I could not express them. In path. I had written my whole paper in 1½ hours; for the rest I sat and corrected, and when I had finished the pages looked like battlefields. I was surprised at myself! I sat there and dried up, cold, a frozen piece of fool.

My number is 28 and if I fail, it will be posted up on the door.

But by Saturday evening I was back at my desk and glad I had not posted the previous four pages of lament because my next letter read thus:

Darling,

By now you have my cable. To my great surprise my number was not on the door. It was, but for my poor double in Physiology. Can you imagine my poor heart! 14 out of 56 failed already – (No. 13 failed both exams). I hope they will make up their quota without poor me. But I will be with you on Wednesday night.

My viva is on Monday a.m. and p.m.. On Tuesday I return the microscope and slides. I will probably not know the result unless I am so bad that they tell me at once.

My large room at Mrs Nelson's (which would have been most enjoyable in summer) was very cold in winter. The small gas fire devoured my shillings with little return of heat. On Sunday, the day before my oral exam, I ran out of my precious shillings. After breakfast, I went fully clothed and gloved to bed, with Dr Scott's microscope perched on my blanket, to peer once more through a new collection of slides.

Unlike my Viennese exams, which had haunted me for years in nightmares, this viva proved to be more of a friendly discussion. I walked out wondering why I had ever been in such a state over it.

During the practical dispensing exams, we were assembled on two sides of a long table. There were about a dozen of us, all busily mixing potions or grinding with pestle and mortar, and kneading the ingredients for pills into neat sausages! These were fitted into the channel of a contraption designed to cut them into ten neat pills. When I was measuring and mixing a cough mixture, an external examiner came to my side and consulted his list of candidates.

"Ah, Dr Stang, you are from Vienna!" Then he murmured several sentences which sounded like gibberish. A hot wave of embarrassment passed through me.

"Sorry, but I... I... do... do not understand the Scottish language," I murmured.

"Oh dear, is my German that bad?" He laughed and I blushed. "Never mind," and he proceeded to discuss my concoction in beautiful Edinburgh English.

Suddenly the examinee opposite decided to cut up his pills and brought down the guillotine with an almighty bang, spraying us with a shower of iron pills. This evoked hilarious laughter all round, while the unlucky candidate scrambled on the floor to retrieve an hour's work.

I did well in my exams and departed with Dr Orr's compliment singing in my ears:

"Many of my Scottish students spell 'dessert' spoon as 'desert' spoon," he added.

This will please Maurice, I thought, who had worked so hard on my spelling. If only I could tell Mama and Papa – but, in an act of self-preservation, I immediately stopped that line of thought.

Chapter Nineteen

Sex Discrimination

I rushed back to Melton Mowbray and into Maurice's arms. This time the wife of the local GP had found some superior digs for me, in which I subsequently spent several weekends.

We had a very pleasant sitting room where I also took my meals. On cool evenings, the landlady, quite unprompted, would light the coal fire. I was served with breakfast and dinner and she included Maurice in a meal whenever he could get away from the camp, even though he had no ration book to give her. At breakfast she always managed a soft boiled egg for me and some meat for dinner. Such luxuries were unknown to me in London, with its severe rationing

I remember my landlady as a strange, tall, good-humoured lady. She was always concerned as to whether her meals were palatable, as she claimed to have lost her faculties of taste and smell after a stroke, which had otherwise left her unharmed.

For special treats there was, of course, the 'Anne of Cleves'. That is where, belatedly, we celebrated Maurice's MA.

I was aglow with my modest success in Edinburgh and was now looking forward to my clinical year. Maurice was sure that he could get to London from wherever he was stationed in the country, while trips to Edinburgh were out of the question. Hence, it had to be London; I had already made my choice of medical school to apply to.

In preparation, I read Sir Henry Tidy's *Synopsis of Medicine,* which in layout resembled my own Viennese clinical notebook which had been lost, along with everything else. For relaxation, I went for walks in the country and day-dreamed of a happy future.

The war over, we would of course find my parents. My dreams varied from my discovering them in a remote Yugoslavian village, to a letter from Leo that they had after all arrived in Palestine, or that they had miraculously escaped and arrived in this country. Some days my fantasies were so vivid that I thought I saw Mother's or Father's head in a crowd and hurried towards the person, only to find myself staring into a stranger's face.

I allowed myself one week of leisure and went to London with a glowing testimonial of my successful pre-clinical exams in my pocket.

Bertha had invited me to stay with her. Her husband Philip was stationed in the Orkneys. She had a three-bedroomed flat at Langbourne Mansions, Holly Lodge Estate in North London. Her younger brother and sister were living with her as they were both still studying in London.

Bertha worked at a firm which produced Polarographs for the analysis of chemical and metal compounds. She had the task of demonstrating them to prospective buyers.

After a lull in the bombing, Hitler's bombers returned in January 1943. The Germans were in Vichy France and enjoying Paris. But there was also the counter-offensive at Stalingrad. This was hailed as proof that the Allies were at last countering the German might.

After supper we sat in front of the electric fire with its three glowing bars, and discussed the past and future into the early hours of the morning. Bertha, in red slacks and stroking back her unruly red hair, spoke for socialism. Becky, in stained dark dungarees, argued, along with her brother, for communism; I, having changed into my shelter slacks to preserve my clothes, was only concerned about a free health service. Sometimes our voices were raised until the neighbours knocked to complain about the disturbance. We could easily be overheard on all sides.

I shared the matrimonial bed with Bertha. A bachelor had the flat overhead. We could follow his footsteps on late nights as he entered his flat, dropped things on the way to the bathroom, pulled the lavatory chain, returned to his bedroom, dropped one shoe and then kept us waiting to drop the other. When we heard his bedsprings creak, we too turned on our sides and went to sleep.

I had set my heart on the Royal Free Hospital. This 'all women' medical school made me feel proud to be in a country where women could set up their own teaching hospital. I obtained an appointment with the Dean – a titled lady. I set out dressed in my Viennese navy blue tailored 'interview suit', with white blouse and bag and gloves to match. I was shown by the porter into a committee room. At the head of a long table sat the lady. She looked up above her moon-shaped reading glasses and bent her head in a polite welcome.

"Miss Stang? Take a seat." She indicated the chair on the right side of the table, and examined my testimonials from Edinburgh, which I had sent in previously.

"Please tell me about your previous experience."

I enumerated my clerkship under Professor Eppinger and my six months work in the pathology department of the Rothschild Hospital in Vienna, after qualification; and, finally, my work in haematology at the Lucas factory.

"Your spoken English is very good," she said.

Then she explained that their intake of students gave priority to 'our girls from Oxford and Cambridge', and then to other English universities. If any places were left, I might be considered.

I pointed out that, unlike the usual undergraduates, I needed only three months in each clinical department, but this appeared to make no difference. I collected my papers, we shook hands and I left.

Bertha found me slumped in my chair in front of the dark electric fire. She switched it on and proceeded to make the tea.

"What does it matter if the Royal Free didn't accept you. There are dozens of medical schools in London."

Next day I called at the Middlesex Hospital and made my way to the medical registrar's office. The man at the reception desk looked at me in surprise.

"But we don't admit women students!"

I couldn't believe I had heard him correctly. "You mean you only accept *male* students?"

"Of course," he answered, as if this would be obvious to any sane person.

In the next few days I phoned Guy's and Bart's, and they too stood by the *male only* principle.

King's and UCH took four women per registration intake and had a waiting list for several years.

REJECTED! As a ten-year-old looking for a grammar school in Vienna, I had been rejected by a headmaster on account of my diminutive size. Mother had found me a school which accepted me after I had passed the entrance exam. No mother now to act for me, I told myself – but put these thoughts out of my mind.

Maurice, on hearing of my failure, arranged for me to come for the weekend to Melton Mowbray. There we decided that I should go and see Dr Macrae at the BMA. He advised me to try the Postgraduate School in Du Cane Road – if this medical school was acceptable to Edinburgh. I spent two days composing the letter to Dr Orr, explaining why I wanted to stay in London until my husband was sent abroad, and then return to Edinburgh for my final exams. I also asked for a recommendation for the Dean of the Postgraduate School. I wrote and re-wrote the letter twice before finally sending it off on Tuesday the 16th of February, 1943. I promised myself not to expect an answer for a week. However, a reply arrived three days later. Such promptitude must herald a refusal. I tore the envelope open.

It contained a sealed letter to the Dean and a friendly note to me. I heaved a sigh of relief but by this time my confidence had sunk to zero. I hesitated to phone for an appointment and finally decided to deliver the precious letter in person. The journey to Du Cane Road took the best part of the morning. I gave the letter to the porter and asked him to take it to the Dean's office and enquire if and when I could have an interview. He returned even before I had time to regret this approach. I was directed to the Dean's office without any further formality.

This time I was in and out of the office before I had fully collected myself. Dr Newman, in a high stiff collar and dark suit, rose behind his desk strewn with books and papers and extended his right hand to me.

"Dr Stang? How do you do? And how is my dear friend Dr Orr?"

I assured him that he was well and running the dispensing courses most effectively.

"He writes that you have done well in your pre-clinicals." I held out my bunch of references, but he took no notice.

"When would you like to start?"

I was too astonished to think.

"As soon as possible."

"Very well, we'll make it the 1st of March – Internal Medicine with Dr MacMichael."

I rushed back to Bertha's, sent a letter to Maurice and the next morning went flat hunting. Bertha recommended the Notting Hill area, "Easy access to Hammersmith Hospital and the underground."

Within the week I had found a one-bedroom flat and given notice to our Balham storage firm; I moved in at the weekend.

Chapter Twenty

Hammersmith Hospital

No. 34 Arundel Gardens was in a row of Georgian houses, most of them having been converted into flats. Seven stone steps led up to each front door, flanked by two slim Tuscan pillars. The ground floor was occupied by a bachelor – an elderly civil servant. Our flat was on the first floor and two elderly school teachers lived above us. The basement and top flat appeared to be empty.

Our rooms were rather cramped. The sitting-room was long and narrow, with the window looking out onto a communal garden to which each flat held a key. A wild vine had crept up the outside wall and its tendrils tried to penetrate the window. The kitchen, dark and doorless, opened off from the sitting-room.

I set out our gateleg table and four chairs near the window. The settee, also known as a 'put-you-up' which opened into a double bed, I lined up against the wall. This was to be for visitors – I still hoped that my parents might suddenly arrive. It stood beside the fire place. I remembered my mother's favourite seat near the tiled stove in Vienna. Our two armchairs faced the hearth, Maurice's within reach of the book-case on the other side.

I opened the cardboard boxes containing our books, doubting that I would be able to arrange them in the right order. No matter. I put Dickens' seventeen volumes on the top shelf and Gibbon's *Decline and Fall of the Roman Empire* on the bottom. Wells' *The History of the World* was one of the first books Maurice had introduced me to. I loved the large, family Bible size of it. I stroked the buff linen binding with its gold lettering and opened it, losing myself for a few moments in the illustrations. Then I realised that Maurice would be here very soon and so I hurriedly returned to filling the shelves. Karl Marx next to Engels. Jespersen, where does he go? More philosophy. Should English, French and German have separate shelves? Maurice would re-arrange them all, and I would love watching him do it. I cleared the boxes out of the way and turned to the kitchen.

I switched on the light and began to stow away our provisions: half a pound of hoarded butter, sugar, precious tea and some pure coffee – the latter was Bertha's contribution. Two boxes of dried egg, breadcrumbs and the inevitable spam. I felt a twinge of conscience. When my parents came, I would throw it, and all the crockery away, and start afresh, being kosher in everything, I consoled myself.

I was still unpacking when the bell rang. Maurice had arrived. We hugged and kissed, overjoyed to be once more in our own home. Every meal prepared with our meagre rations seemed a feast.

After six months in Melton Mowbray, Maurice was moved to Kennett, near Newmarket. It was a holding camp prior to going abroad. Discipline was relaxed and Maurice was sure he would be home more frequently.

In February, thirty-five thousand German soldiers had surrendered at Stalingrad and the RAF had bombed Berlin.

"Who knows, it may all be over soon and I won't even be sent abroad," Maurice told me.

There was a three-day debate in Parliament on the National Health Service; I followed it closely and blessed those stars which had guided me to this country. I dreamed of a rosy dawn once the war was over. I shall work in a health service that is free to all, I thought. The Luftwaffe was still dropping bombs on London, but here the sounds were muted and I never had to seek shelter in the basement.

On Monday, 1st March, 1943, I presented myself at the Hammersmith Hospital. The porter who registered my attendances showed me up to the ward. There, Dr MacMichael was about to start a ward round. He acknowledged my arrival with a slight nod. There were about a dozen of us, but only one other female. Afterwards, she came up to me and introduced herself as Dr Hilda Abraham. She was the daughter of the deceased Professor Karl Abraham, a psychoanalyst and well known authority on melancholia, and a close friend of Professor Freud. The men were all post-graduate students from Guy's and Bart's. The two groups hardly communicated with each other, and nobody spoke to us. Dr MacMichael too, paid little attention to the two foreign, female interlopers.

Dr Abraham was a tall redhead with expressive blue eyes, an attractive smile and strong capable hands. Her handwriting was curiously large and she wrote her notes very slowly and deliberately. She was preparing to follow in her father's footsteps as a psychoanalyst. She had qualified as an MD in Berlin, but like me felt the need to re-qualify once she had decided to remain in this country. She was encouraged by Anna Freud and had the close support of Dr Lantos, a Hungarian psychoanalyst in whose house she lived.

We became lifelong friends. After lectures, we often returned to my flat to prepare inventive meals from our meagre rations, discuss endlessly and engage in study. This friendship and the thought of Maurice coming home every Saturday on the 1.05 train from Newmarket made my term in internal medicine bearable.

On Sunday 16th May, we woke to the sounds of a cuckoo and church bells ringing in the African victory of the Allies. With new hopes in our hearts we celebrated at Lyons Corner House on Tottenham Court Road. The fare was kippers – which were served only after 10 p.m.!

I started my second term in the surgical ward. By now Hilda and I were hardened to the fact that we were ignored; hence our surprise when, on turning up in Outpatients, Professor Grey Turner greeted us as welcome newcomers. He had spent some time in Vienna before the First World War, where he had visited hospitals and mixed with the students.

"Do the students still congregate in the cafés, to study and chat, and sit for hours over one cup of coffee and a *Kipferl*?" (the crescent shaped roll of Vienna.)

"Yes," I laughed at his detailed recollection.

"And do the waiters still provide a glass of your excellent Viennese water with the coffee?"

"Yes, and they even replace the empty glass with fresh water." After a second's hesitation, I added: "At least, they did so when I was last there." He had known my professors when they were young aspiring surgeons. Then he questioned me more seriously on the history of medicine. I was grateful that Maurice had selected Singer's *History of Medicine* for me, which I had read in the British Museum Reading Room.

Professor Turner was a short man and somewhat neglectful in dress. Once, passing him outside the hospital, I had hardly recognised him with his large head hidden under an old bowler hat.

One day we watched him at a four hour operation removing a diseased kidney. The next morning he held an early outpatients' session. We assembled in the white room with its examination couch, instrument trolley, eye-chart and reflecting mirror on the opposite wall. The desk below the window held a block of notepaper and the first patient's clinical notes in their buff folder. As he opened the folder, Professor Turner explained that the patient was a Miss Haigh. We had seen him remove her melanoma of the right cheek and we had debated, after she had left, if it should be followed up with irradiation.

"The glands are not yet invaded. If we are lucky, she can escape further damage to her face. She is only twenty-nine!" 'My age,' I thought.

The nurse announced, "Miss Haigh is in the waiting room."

"Please show her in," the Professor said.

A slim, pale, mousey young woman with a scarf over her head, hiding half her face, followed the nurse into the surgery.

"Good morning, Miss Haigh." The professor greeted her and pointed to the chair near the trolley where the nurse had positioned herself. Miss Haigh removed her scarf and looked shyly up at us. I smiled at her, hoping to reassure her. Her hair was tightly rolled in a crescent round her head. The nurse snipped off the dressing, revealing a red line in front of her right ear. The scar reached down below the jaw. Professor Turner sat down opposite her.

"It is healing well. You have good healing power," he complimented her. He felt round the scar and the neck for tell-tale glands, then nodded, satisfied; so we knew he had felt no glands.

"You can now leave the dressing off," he told her and then turned to us. "How can we disguise the scar, which will fade, of course, but...?"

We crowded round, but before anybody had been able to suggest anything, he had found the solution.

"Let's see! Can you let your hair down?" Miss Haigh removed the band and her straight, blonde hair fell down to her shoulders.

"What work do you do?" he asked.

"I am a typist."

"Splendid! I was afraid you might be working near machinery. Look!" He got up and pointed to the mirror reflecting the eye chart.

She stood up and blushed as she looked at her image. The scar was no longer visible.

Arrangements were made for her check-ups. She shook hands with us all and left, swinging her scarf, a smiling image of Veronica Lake.

We were only a handful of students here and we all adored Professor Turner. He made surgery a truly humane art.

On returning home from the clinic on Thursday 9th September, I found Maurice waiting for me on the doorsteps waving a cheque. It was our fourth wedding anniversary and his father had sent him a cheque for two hundred pounds.

"Isn't it nice of the old man? And I have the weekend off and Italy has surrendered." He laughed. "We must celebrate with a present for you! Now you need no longer worry about your fees."

We went to Etam's in Oxford Street and Maurice selected a long red quilted dressing gown for three pounds, which I thought a terrible extravagance.

"That will keep you warm when you have to hurry through the long draughty corridors in the small hours."

I bought him a Swan fountain pen. "This will encourage you to write daily." He had complained that he often could not find a pen in his camp.

The following week I started my third clinical term in the obstetric and gynaecology department. I had excitedly told Hilda that the consultant was a woman. We assembled in front of the ante-natal ward on our first morning.

"*Mein Gott!*" Hilda whispered. I turned and saw a white-coated woman of indiscernible age, stern-faced, and followed by a similarly white-coated cocker spaniel with black leggings. As he trotted along behind her, he flapped his long black earlobes. He was followed by Sister.

Our little group received a curt greeting, then she turned to the dog. "Sit!" she said, and we proceeded into the ward. When we left, the dog got up and followed her. I was later told by Sister that he guarded her every footstep, including when she had to visit the toilet, but would wait patiently outside wards and operating theatres.

Alas, two weeks later Maurice came home on embarkation leave. I sneaked away from my clinics as soon as my presence had been registered.   We went to cinemas and theatres trying to forget the pending separation.   We discussed only my studies and my plans to work for at least a year in hospitals before settling into general practice.

"Cod-liver oil and orange juice are now supplied free of charge for babies.   It's the start of a free health service."   I was full of enthusiasm.   But the days passed only too quickly.

"Let me come with you until you have to leave the camp!" I begged.

"No, I want to leave you with your studies and your friends."

We said goodbye at Liverpool Street station.   I saw Maurice swallowed up in a pool of khaki and, as I had promised, I left before the train started.   I still avoid that station to this day.

On Monday, 15th November, 1943, it was so foggy that Dr Hilda Abraham and I decided to leave the Hammersmith Hospital early in the afternoon.   Hilda had a long way to get back to Primrose Hill.

I got off the bus into the uncanny silence of the thickening fog.   It descended like a wet, grey blanket, muffling all noise of traffic and footsteps.   The air reeked of soot and sulphur. The policeman at the crossing was slowly blocked out.   First his head and arms disappeared, then his body and finally his legs and boots.

As I turned into Arundel Gardens, I could just see only the first of the seven steps leading to each front door of the houses.   I counted all the even numbers to thirty-four from number eight at the corner.   Once inside, I switched on the blue-tinted electric light in the hall and climbed to the first floor.   As I unlocked the door I caught sight of a postcard on the mat.   It was Maurice's last will and testament, an officially printed card filled in by every soldier going abroad.

He had left England; this was expected, but nevertheless a shock.   I shivered and went to light the fire in the grate, crouching in front of it on the rug.   Chin on knees, I watched it slowly flame up, and fed it small pieces of coal as I had been taught to do.   Little sparks spat from their pockets of primeval gas and finally it started to glow.

I imagined myself on the ship with Maurice.   I wanted to follow him in my mind, to be near him.   I reached for a book at random on the bottom shelf of the bookcase next to the fireplace.

It was the second volume of the pocket edition of Gibbon's *Decline and Fall*.   Maurice would approve of such erudite reading.   Perhaps it would even improve my scrappy knowledge of ancient history.

In front of the book was a map: 'The Roman Empire in AD 180'. I could trace the way from Britannia, along the coasts of France and Spain to North Africa, where we had guessed he would be going. On page three, I read of the 'religious harmony of the ancient world...' and that '... even hostile nations embraced or at least respected each others' superstitions.' What a different view this was of the Romans from Caesar's *De Bello Gallico*, which had plagued me throughout a year in grammar school!

The fire's exuberance was short lived. Giant grey fingers of fog reached down the chimney and choked the warm glow, making a shiver run down my spine.

A bad omen! I shook myself. Was I becoming superstitious? I got up, my stomach grumbling. I had forgotten to eat, so I swallowed a cup of milk and went to bed.

Maurice had promised to write as soon as it was possible to send letters. I was going to be sensible. However, I slept fitfully, plagued by nightmares, and woke to a grey morning.

I got up, drank some of the milk the faithful milkman had left at my door and went back to bed.

"I will stay here until his letter comes," I decided, and for two days I did just that. On the third day Hilda came hammering at my door. I pretended not to hear, but she had guessed. She shouted through the keyhole. "Do you want me to call the police and have them break the door down? I'll do it, you know!"

I opened the door and she proceeded to shake me out of the torpor that had enveloped me.

"You know you can't expect any post for at least one month or more. He is in transit and soldiers are not allowed to send letters until they land." Of course I knew. This was a measure taken to prevent post falling into enemy hands and thus giving away the location of troops at sea. Maurice had told me all this before he left.

Hilda assured me that she wouldn't allow me to neglect the obligatory attendance at the clinic and lose a term and delay my finals.

Every morning as I closed the door of our flat, a part of me stayed behind to wait for the air letter. Returning, I tried not to look for it on the mat.

I did not take up Gibbon again, but buried myself in medical textbooks.

The days were long, and the nights even longer. I took out bundles of previous letters and read them in bed, pretending they had just arrived. I fell asleep, exhausted, and was woken by nightmares.

I resolved not to read the newspapers and I had no radio. But I could not prevent my eyes from scanning the headlines of the papers my fellow passengers were reading in the bus. One headline – 'CONVOY ATTACKED' – set my heart hammering until I read on to discover that it had been an Atlantic food convoy. At the bus stop I closed my eyes. 'If I count to three and my bus comes in view, there will be a letter.' I immediately told myself off for such childish games.

It was mid-December when, gathering for the outpatient session, I heard two students discussing the death of the consultant's husband. He had just been killed in action. My heart contracted. When she came in she was clearly distraught. She looked at us blankly and said to nobody in particular, "Some people come here and live in safety, while we get ourselves killed in an effort to defend them!"

I grabbed my coat and bag off the hook and left, running for the bus and home, while I could still control my tears. I opened the door and sank down next to the airmail letter on the mat.

Chapter Twenty-One

Edinburgh

Maurice's letters became my lifeline. We had agreed to number them. When none arrived for a few days I was frantic. Then three or four arrived and I put them in chronological order before reading them. When possible we both wrote every day. Each night I took a bunch to bed with me to re-read and finally fall asleep with them resting on Maurice's pillow.

The seventh letter which had reached me first was undated:

> *Draft RDFYK APO 5770*
>
> *Darling,*
>
> *For some hours after dinner I lay down and enjoyed the rich man's delicacy of sun out of season – the sky is blue and the sun strong, though still a trifle wintry, and a ghost of a moon swings up aloft. A contrast to yesterday when I was feeling so sick that I missed yet another letter. I wish I could send you the pleasant things in conserves. My 'furor legendi' has abated. I have been unlucky with my books and yesterday I couldn't read at all...*

I guessed he had been sea-sick. Had he now landed? This was confirmed in his tenth letter – the others had been lost.

> *November 28th, 1943.*
>
> *Darling,*
>
> *You must be in a fever of impatience. So am I. Well, at last we are allowed to date our letters. We are in a place. What a place! None of the letters would have reached you before this one – circumstances were exceptional. Anyhow, letters coming from you ought to be better and I am frantic for an airgraph or a letter.*

This was the start of fairly regular post. Maurice was very careful not to give the censor any excuse to blot out his writing; nevertheless, an opportunity apparently arose in the following:

> *... I am conscious I did not do enough for you. If I helped you in your career you have repaid me a thousandfold in five years of happiness. You remember the story of XXXXXXX*

(blotted out by the censor)

> *prince who said he'd not had above 9 days of happiness in his existence – so I am a very lucky man...*

In his next letter he complained thus:

> *... I can't tell you what I feel with the censor perched like an evil bird on my left shoulder, so you'll have to gather that I love you in a hopeless way from the hints I drop coyly in the course of my letters! It is most embarrassing. I wish we had been more demonstrative lovers in cinemas, parks and public places – then I wouldn't be so shy now.*

Poor Maurice! I felt the same and so we went on discussing the books he was reading and I told him about my work in the hospital.

A week later the winter term finished and the Dean duly certified my attendance for the three terms. I had served my time and had no regrets at leaving and completing my fourth term in Edinburgh. I was, however, still short of a course in vaccination, when, quite by chance, I passed Paddington Hospital and noticed a poster offering a vaccination course.

It was due to start at 11 a.m. The time by my little watch (smuggled through the Nazi post in a packet of dates) was 10.30. I promptly followed a couple of officers into a small lecture room where Dr Himmelwhite (a fellow refugee) gave us an hour's talk. We then went with him into a surgery to carry out the prescribed vaccinations.

Two drops of vaccine were placed half an inch apart on the upper arm. The choice of arm was left to the patient. Two very shallow quarter inch incisions were made through each drop with a small stiletto-like needle which was flamed over a spirit light to make it sterile. The art here was not to cut too deeply so as to draw blood, yet deeply enough for the vaccine to penetrate.

As I stuck a dressing over my patient's arm, I reminded him not to get it wet.

"No fear, in three inches of bath water I can hardly get my backside wet!"

"Please come back in a week to check if it has taken and get your certificate. The arm may be a bit sore," I added as an afterthought.

"I hope it doesn't swell up like my brother's. Looked like a blooming balloon, it did!"

But when, a week later, I saw my patient again there were two neat blisters. Dr Himmelwhite inspected the masterpiece and signed both our certificates. I put a fresh dressing on the arm and advised him to remove it in a week to ten days. I was now a qualified vaccinator and went to the office to pay my fee of fifteen shillings.

The man at the small office window looked at me in surprise.

"You can't have done the course here!"

I waved the blue official document at him as proof before replacing it securely in my bag.

"But we don't take ladies on our courses!" he muttered, quite upset. I smiled at him. "And I can't enter your name in my book!" With that he went to the back of the office and summoned a colleague. They conferred in whispers. When he came back, I felt quite sorry for him. After all, he hadn't made the rules.

"Enter me as Francis with an 'i'," I suggested.

But he shook his head and pushed the ten shilling note and two half crowns towards me. Another colleague approached to pay, so I cashed the money and left.

I sublet my flat to a pleasant young couple, who promised to look after it for me and paid me one month in advance. I wrote to Maurice and told him to direct his letters to Bertha, who would send them on as soon as I had a settled address in Edinburgh.

At the beginning of the second week in January, 1944, I stepped once more out of Waverley Station into a frosty Princes Street. I was weighed down by a suitcase containing my winter and summer clothes and a parcel of six heavy medical books. Setting my case down, I took a deep breath of fresh air and looked at the charming street before me.

A young man coming up behind me put his hand under the handle of my suitcase and asked, "May I carry this for you?"

Surprised, I looked up into a youthful smiling face under dark curly hair. A tartan scarf was wound round his neck, trailing over a heavy tweed coat. He certainly didn't look like a porter.

"I am a Scout," he explained, "and this will be my good deed for the day." He lifted the heavy case with ease. "Where are you bound for?"

"The Surgeon's Hall," I replied, smiling.

"Splendid, that isn't much out of my way."

'This is a good beginning,' I thought, as we walked along chatting. I was glad to be sitting my exams here and not in London.

I went straight to the office to register. The secretary, who remembered me, enquired if I had digs and handed me a list of approved lodgings with the comment, "I am afraid we are absolutely full up, but I hope you can find somewhere to stay!"

But I felt full of confidence and went to the telephone booth to ring Mrs Nelson.

"Oh, it's you," came the familiar voice. "Why didn't you let me know six months ago that you were coming back? I am now fully booked until the summer break, my dear."

I went to the café nearby, bought a cup of tea and collected sufficient pennies for twelve calls. Starting at the top of the list, the first four were all fully booked. 'I am a fool,' I thought, 'of course, everybody starts at the top of the column.' At the bottom was a name in ink, obviously recently added – a Mrs Farlan.

"Yes, I have a room to spare in my new bungalow," came a friendly young voice. "It's not fully furnished yet, but I am getting it together. Would you like to see it?" She spelled out the address for me to write down. At my request to move in straight away, she asked: "Do you know Edinburgh? Where are you now?"

"I am at the telephone booth near the Surgeon's Hall. Do you know it?"

A peal of laughter followed my question.

"I know every telephone booth in Edinburgh. I work on the lines. I'll pick you up at ten minutes past five. Is that all right?"

I had an hour to wait. On my way back to the café, I passed a newspaper stand and stopped to read the headlines:

RUSSIANS OPEN NEW OFFENSIVE IN
NW AND SW OF LENINGRAD AND N OF
NOVGOROD

and another:

US TROOPS TAKE MONTE TROCCHO

I wished I had taken our world atlas with me. Perhaps Mrs Farlan
had one.

Over another cup of tea, I finished the letter to Maurice, which I
had started in the train, and sent a postcard to Bertha giving her my
new address.

I was woken the next morning by an elderly, plump woman in a
Fair Isle jumper and tartan skirt, secured at the side with a giant safety
pin. She deposited a large cup of dark tea on the small table next to the
sumptuous double bed I was in.

"I am Nanny," she announced. "You wanted to be woken at 7.30.
I lit you a fire. You Southerners aren't used to our fresh cold winter
mornings."

She had drawn the curtains of the two tall windows to my left,
letting in some grey light. I found I was in a large, all-white, furnished
master bedroom. Opposite the bed was a palatial fireplace with a lusty
fire burning in it.

"Did you sleep well? You were certainly dead to the world when I
came in to light the fire."

I raised my head and managed a croaky, "Yes, thank you, thank
you."

"We are in the breakfast room," was her parting shot.

My head sank back on the pillow. I dozed and dreamed that
Maurice and I were on holiday. I stretched out my hand and touched
the ice cold linen of the empty pillow. Now I was fully awake.
Maurice was in North Africa, Leo in a Kibbutz in Palestine, and my
parents, my parents were...? I looked round in surprise at my
luxurious surroundings.

From the high ceiling hung an alabaster lampshade, glowing pink
from the reflected light of the fire. My eyes swept down towards the
mantelpiece. Above it was a life-size painting of a seated beauty
dressed as a gypsy. Her large shawl, strewn with red roses and bright
green leaves, was draped over one shoulder. There was a faint

resemblance to... I took a few sips of the scalding tea which woke me to full consciousness. I remembered: the painting was a flattering portrait of Mrs Farlan's sister, whom I had met the previous night.

I now also remembered the little group of newly built bungalows where Mrs Farlan had taken me. She had been dressed in a dark trouser suit resembling some uniform. She had arrived punctually, but out of breath, at ten past five. She was a few inches taller than I, rosy cheeked with short cut straight black hair and smiling eyes. We took an immediate liking to each other. We had entered a hall cluttered with crates. She led the way to the smaller of two bedrooms and deposited my suitcase in the room which contained just a bare bedstead.

"We shall sleep at my sister's tonight. By tomorrow I shall have it all ship-shape. My husband's friend will help me." She indicated the crates in the hall.

On January 17th, 1944, I entered on my final prescribed clinical quarter. Lectures had started when I arrived. I tiptoed into the theatre by the back door and slipped into the last row. As I peered down over the heads I saw a student listening to the chest of a patient sitting up in a hospital bed. X-rays were clipped on the illuminated panels next to it.

The lecturer, a middle-aged man in a white coat, asked him, "... and vot vould you prescribe?" He rolled his 'r's. I was no longer interested in the patient. A foreign accent! He was of medium height, round-faced, of ruddy complexion. His dark hair, parted on one side, was greying at the temples. He was repeatedly rubbing his wrists – I later learned that he suffered from psoriasis. A Continental! Not German, perhaps Polish? No, I decided; Russian or some other Slav nationality.

At the end of the lecture, I went down and introduced myself and learned that he was Dr Oscar Olbrich from Prague and that he had passed the same exams as I was to do, a few years earlier. He advised me what lectures to attend, patted my shoulder, and smiled.

"You vill like it here, Dr Shtung."

And 'Shtung' I remained, although everybody else pronounced my name correctly.

I soon got to know the other lecturers and learned that Dr Olbrich was highly thought of. The atmosphere was a relaxed one. The obstetrician, for instance, held a weekly 'at home' for his students, to which I as a newcomer was immediately invited.

I settled down to lectures during the morning and went back to my medical books in the afternoon, with letter writing in the evening. Maurice wrote as regularly, and even included teaching sessions in spelling.

> ... *I have a bone to pick with you – spelling. It is carelessness, I suppose, but do you think 'suxessful' is the King's English or 'hugh' will do for 'huge'? Really now! I suggest you compare a page of your notes with the text book daily, and scrutinise the spelling! Improve or I will get nasty! That is an Order, as they say in the army. The light has just gone out.*

I thought there must be somebody on my side, but the next day it was continued:

> *Well, I have applied, but my chances of getting into the interpreter's school are thin. I did write you I wanted a couple of grammars.* Ripman's Rapid French *and* Rapid Italian *courses. They will probably be second-hand but may have been reprinted lately. Send them singly. If it will worry you and isn't easy to get, then forget it. What I need even more are photos, mementoes of you.*
> *Another crop of spelling errors. You are confusing 'd's with 't's, 'v's with 'f's. You write 'life' instead of 'live', 'sent' instead of 'send', and vice versa! You surely don't make those mistakes in your pronunciation? For heaven's sake, beware!*

And then he finished the letter with love and kisses.

Chapter Twenty-Two
Letters and Exams

Mrs Farlan and I became good friends, although we never addressed each other by our first names; indeed, I don't remember ever knowing her Christian name. I soon learned that she was not over-fond of her older sister, whom she thought a snob.

"... with her officer husband, her twin boys and nanny," she would mutter when the subject came up.

However, she adored her mother-in-law and we often visited her and always got a 'wholesome' meal. She was a large-bosomed Scottish 'mum' with greying hair gathered up in a bun on top of her head. She went to 'kirk' on Sundays, advised us on sensible housekeeping and addressed me after the first formal introduction as her 'wee lassie'. They were a rather tall family. Her son, Mrs Farlan's husband, was in the air force and his wife communicated with him by means of unauthorised telephone calls, as she knew all the operators along the route. They never wrote to each other.

By the end of February, rumour had it that the Japanese were ill-treating their prisoners. I was glad Maurice was in North Africa, although in his letter he complained:

> *Still no word from you. I am in despair. I am spending a melancholy Saturday, alone and with nothing particularly in view, in the city, which, in spite of its crowds and varied scenes, can be very arid. I stood it up to five o'clock but I could stand it no longer. Off I went to the YMCA, exchanged my cap for a bottle of ink, took a nib out of my cigarette case and a pen from my breast-pocket and started this letter to the only being in the world I care for.*

I was distressed as I had written daily. I also noticed that he had lost his fountain pen. Still, Japan would be worse, especially as on the last page he consoled me with:

> *However, miserable as I am, I can still spend a little time rummaging in the bookshops. This time I bought, in my favourite tuppenny-ha'penny edition, a copy of two little volumes of Goethe's* Iphigenie *in the original. I only had to read the first speech for the memories to come flooding back of when I first encountered the play. How tranquil the play is in itself, though. And how like the French classical plays I have been reading lately. There is no Shakespearean influence worth mentioning in* Iphigenie. *I'll read it and imagine you are listening in the armchair opposite. Yes, sometimes I look up from my book and await your comments, forgetting you are many hundreds of miles away. etc...*

Yes, we were lucky. We could converse, even across all those miles as if sitting next to each other in the privacy of our study. But I was furious with the end of the letter. Maurice wrote:

> *From North Africa I send you my love and kisses. I hope they will reach you without undue delay in that grey northern city of yours.*
>
> *Love, Maurice.*

There followed an indecipherable and intrusive signature – that of the censor.

By the end of the Easter term I had completed my clinical year and could start on my exams. The first half was to take place in Edinburgh and the second in Glasgow, for which I would get an additional string of letters.

Everyone here was so friendly and appreciative of my knowledge that I started full of confidence. And then it happened: I failed the exam in obstetrics! The reason escapes me. I can only recollect getting into some controversy with my examiner, an absolutely idiotic thing to do.

I dashed for the bus and as I trudged up the hill I was glad to find that Mrs Farlan was still out. I sat down to pour out my woes to

Maurice: *'I have let you down...'* I started, and I felt in addition that I had let down all refugee students.

Everybody was very sympathetic. Mrs Farlan tried to persuade me to come dancing with her, convinced I had overworked and needed distraction.

Dr Olbrich assured me, "... it happens in the best families."

Bertha commiserated with me and Hilda wrote that she had failed surgery for the second time and missed me very much. To Leo, working in his kibbutz, I wrote only that I was still working hard on my exams. There was no need to worry him, too.

Next day a letter arrived from Maurice:

> *Today, looking through my stuff, I took our double photograph out of the exercise book I keep it in. It gave me a pang to see your sweet little face and to think that all your sweetness is 'wasted on the desert air'. I feel myself melting with yearning for you. My body makes a positive effort to reach you. I try to imagine our reunion. I'll spend days just listening to your voice. I'll sit and listen to you reading – what? Goethe's* Iphigenie, *I think. I looked at it again the other day. 'Seeking the land of the Greeks with the soul' – just expresses my feelings if you substitute for 'the land of the Greeks' with just one wonderful, inimitable little individual. And we'll read Schiller for old times' sake. I wonder if we'll be just a little bit shy of each other? So that we could fall in love again and start from the beginning with a real honeymoon and many kisses.*

> *Your Maurice.*

Tears of longing trickled down my cheek. I walked out into the garden. A slight green flush covered the bare branches of the trees and here and there a golden crocus smiled at me. Far off on the horizon, silvery white, lace-edged waves danced on the darkening sea. A salty breeze announced spring. Dusk called me back to my books to put in another hour before supper.

Suddenly no letter for a whole week. I would run down the slope to catch the postman before he started to walk up the garden path to each bungalow. The eighth and ninth day passed and still no army airmail.

Even the postman was upset by now. At last, on the tenth day, he waved the letter at me from afar, marked with the black censor's stamp.

I stopped to read:

My sweet darling,

Forgive the silence, forgive the pencil; the excuse for both is that I am in Italy. (Yes, I am actually allowed to tell you that!) The journey was humdrum and uneventful. Apart from the general discomfort, I might have been a tourist.

Anyhow, the consolation is that I am a good deal nearer home, geographically speaking. Can't tell you anything about the country yet; I'll probably like it and find, to my gratification, that my Italian is better than I had expected. I like the way the vines are laced between fruit trees in rows, and another crop is grown on the ground. The method allows three different products on the same bit of earth – it is a sort of garden agriculture evolved, no doubt, as a result of the scarcity of land.

I notice I am one of only two men writing home in a whole tentful dozing away after the journey. So I can claim to be a devoted husband.

I jumped on the bus after reading this first page. Italy! Maurice was coming nearer home.

'Italy,' I almost sang aloud. All was well with my world.

Now letters became much more regular and frequent. Mrs Farlan loved it when I read her passages which she claimed were better than a novel.

A week after Easter we received a box of almonds and the following letter, which we both enjoyed:

I've been a very busy man recently. I am doing some clerking work for the unit temporarily, and will probably, in addition, run a course in the Italian language. The work is quite interesting and of course much more in my line than what I have been doing so far. The last three days have seen me in very good humour.

Just before dinner today I received 2 belated air letters from you, dated 6 and 8 of Feb. You must have forgotten their contents, but I could positively hear your voice as I read them. All your letters, even your most casual notes written while waiting in a lecture room or in a pause in your studies, seem full of your personality. I am very satisfied with you as a correspondent...

Further down came something which aroused my curiosity:

Yesterday, the bath parade took me near a very interesting place, a walled Italian town. The entire place is encircled by a wall in a fair state of preservation, though parts of it have been incorporated into houses, parts are broken down and nearly all of it is crowned with vegetation. Some of the towers are perfectly preserved and the portals (which are now without gates) seem to invite one into the Middle Ages. The invitation must be resisted because for some unknown reason the place is out of bounds.

I asked around in the college and one colleague, who had travelled in Italy before the war, suggested it might be Lucca, a town near Pisa. I was delighted to see it was so far North – nearer home. 'One day we might visit it together,' I day-dreamed.

A few days later two letters arrived marked 50(a) and 50(b), which Mrs Farlan and I could enjoy in their entirety.

Whackett and myself continue to act as unofficial interpreters. Some of our jobs are surprising and even embarrassing – the things soldiers want to have translated!
Easter is upon us and I am trying to hold off the memories of the ones we spent together in the traditional manner. I seem to see the dazzling white cloth spread with symbolical dishes and dainties. The one we had at No.13 in the days of our poverty was the best. The one we spent with Phil and Bertha comes second maybe, but a long way behind.
The weather is warm and many of the dainty little fruit trees are already in blossom. The Italian peasants are celebrating their Easter in the traditional manner. The pathetic corpses of lambs (the Paschal Lamb) are hanging

in the butchers' shops. The woman in the house adjoining our cookhouse killed a lamb the day before yesterday. And in lieu of Easter eggs, which are not known here, housewives are baking cakes and pizza. Ah, but you know nothing about this Italian dish! It is a kind of bread cake with a filling. We have tasted (euphemism – we ate huge chunks) three types of pizza with fillings of pickled tomatoes, vegetables and cheese and egg respectively. It tastes best eaten hot.

Mrs Farlan and I puzzled over this unknown dish. 'Pizza', it sounded so funny. We munched some more almonds and I continued to read.

We had two Easter dinners yesterday. We ate the first in the poor room of our laundress, but the food was delightful and tasty, and the welcome warm. I provided the dessert by treating the assembled company to – ice cream! I can see you wince, you poor thing. Can you picture me going for the ice-cream, flanked by two eager children? There is a delightful little girl of 10 whose immense energies pour into a thousand channels. Within five minutes you have her playing, doing the courtesies of the household, running with the jug to fetch the water or wine or walnuts, keeping the frying pan going on the little charcoal stove, rocking the baby, stopping the little boy (a fool, of course) from playing with the cutlery laid out for the visitors, taking the place of her mother whenever necessary and continuing to be a real, natural, healthy Italian child, screaming with laughter at the slightest pretext. We get on very well, for as you know I am an ardent feminist, convinced of the superiority of women in all things. I have taught her an Italian nursery rhyme! Her mother, with her worn, thin face, is an example of what may happen to this charming creature unless of course you want to adopt her. Anyhow, Clegg (cook, intelligent, interested in lingoes) and I had a delightful meal. We stayed to about 6.30 when we left to appear for our second invitation of the day.

A farmhouse this time, belonging to a prosperous family of peasants. Their parlour is large and airy, floored with rough stone it is true, but provided with such luxuries as a radio and a Singer sewing machine. We sit around the semicircular hearth watching the brushwood crackle. Yesterday, there was an iron rest over the fire supporting a great vessel of water into which went handfuls of the finest spaghetti I have ever seen. The whole family debated the point at which the spaghetti could be declared cooked. As we'd had a whole dish of spaghetti already, we couldn't really do justice to it all. We sat there for the evening drinking a red wine which leaves a dry, not unpleasant taste in the mouth, while the old peasant drank our beer (which he preferred) and smoked a long-stemmed pipe. It is a nice family, but with just a trace of reserve which makes it so different from the other. The grandmother sits close to the fire, the old crone of the fairy tales, dressed in a black hood, crocheting or drinking her one solace, cocoa. There are three charming daughters. (don't worry, they are all married or bespoken), but the nicest is the eldest, a woman with greying hair, the sweetest and kindliest of faces; she has three children including a girl of 13. Her husband came down for the Easter holidays on leave and I fell in love with him. He speaks the richest, roundest, fullest, most musical Italian I have ever heard, a charming personality too. The second daughter is usually away on another farm (between them they have half a dozen). The youngest is a very typical Italian girl, works very hard, makes excellent cocoa, isn't too strong on spelling (for which reason I rather like her) and is engaged to the usual film star type. The old man sometimes sets his bed alight with his pipe (he combats insomnia with two pipefuls per night). She excuses him, saying 'old people are like children – they must have their little pleasures'. It sounded brutal, although it was kindly meant, a sad statement in fact. I shall now start on another airletter to tell you how much I love and miss you.

Chapter Twenty-Three

Scabies

"I bet you won't read me the next one," Mrs Farlan said teasingly. I looked up and noticed my friend scratching her hands.

"They have been so itchy the last few days. My body too," she complained.

I made her stand under the lamp.

"You have caught scabies. Where did you sleep the other night, when you were on duty?"

"I borrowed a sleeping bag from one of the girls."

"You'd better warn her. She probably has it, too."

"I thought only tramps got it," she replied mournfully.

"You must go and see your doctor. He will give you a lotion to rub in after a bath each evening. You will need fresh pyjamas to change into each time. It will take about a week to get rid of it."

It did take a week. Mrs Farlan ran out of her own pyjamas and used her husband's. On the following Sunday they were dancing in the breeze on the washing line. Her scabies was cured but our neighbours turned their heads away when we passed. There were not even any 'good mornings' for us. Our reputation was in shreds.

However, we had a good laugh when we told Mac, Mrs Farlan's husband's friend and our self-appointed minder. I myself did not care a jot as long as the postman continued to bring me Maurice's letters. Their inimitable style made up for everything.

> *...I want you to forgive me for the absurd tourist nonsense I tend to write in my pedantic airmails; it is just the result of the constraint of the censorship; I really don't want to bore you with descriptions of peasant life in Italy...*

*Don't be afraid of my sitting in front of the fire
reading Schiller or any other bore all the time...*

*Or would you like to relive the time in Melton
Mowbray with dear old Mrs Brown and egg and honey
for breakfast? Or housekeeping days in Kensington? I
can close my eyes and picture you standing there on top
of my big Bible, trying to make yourself taller. As if I
didn't prefer you as a little girl of 5 foot. Just remain my
little tot and I'll be happy. Or will you be naughty and
perverse, lying on the cushions on Bertha's divan, paying
no attention to me? I'll forgive you, of course.*

I assured Maurice that I loved to hear about Italy and that I was still
re-reading his Easter story and enjoying it.

*...The other day I made a great effort and constructed a
bed out of packing case wood. It is a great improvement
and serves as bed, desk and chair. The real incentive
was my discovery one morning of a lovely land crab that
had apparently kept me company all night! It was about
three inches across and had formidable looking pincers.
I decided there and then to get off the ground. I also
have a 'bookcase' containing a miniature library, a very
respectable one too. I found half a dozen French novels
in the Quartermaster's store and was told I could keep
them. Do you remember a little piece I translated once
from the French – about the growing eccentricities of an
old woman? Well, there was a novel of the writer of that
piece, François Mauriac. Quite good. I devoured it two
Sundays ago.*

*I am nervous of reading in my tent now at night as we
sleep under mosquito netting.*

*When I write about the books I have read, don't think
I am forgetting to dream of you for one instant. You are
always floating through my mind and I am discussing the
books with you all the time.*

*I am afraid you might not always appreciate the book.
My last one was Thierry's* History *of the Norman
Conquest of England – I finished it at dinner time today –
it would have done your English history knowledge good.*

How silly I am. I shall go back to my tent and dream of our weekends in Melton, in the sitting room before the fire, in our bedroom in Kensington, in Bertha's flat and lots of other places.

Mrs Farlan wanted to hear the story of the old woman, but alas I couldn't remember the details.

A few days later I made an unexpected find in my bookshop which I thought Maurice would really like to have – I waited impatiently to hear if it had reached him. After two weeks, I started to count the days, and then his reply came:

Darling,

Yesterday I came back tired and dusty from an interview about an interpreter's post and had a most welcome surprise waiting for me on my bed. A letter dated the 10th, a packet containing Hogben's Interglossa *and another with a newspaper dated the 7th. Magnificent!*

My sweet girl, love works wonders! You with your lack of book sense (congenital or acquired) to be able to pick out what would interest, stimulate or provoke your unreasonable husband with his unaccountable fads! A great achievement! Interglossa *has set me thinking; it has reminded me of my philological days when I was deep in the study of Jespersen and most of all it is a concrete proof of the way you keep me in mind, and though I don't need proof, still it is very sweet.*

The interview was none too promising and I was told transfer would be a leisurely process; and among the questions was one about the nationality of my parents...

'Darling Maurice,' I thought, 'sparing me the question about the nationality of his wife – an enemy alien.' As his parents were immigrants from Eastern Europe, he hardly stood a chance of getting the posting.

I took up a job for two hours every morning assisting a married couple of austere-looking scientists. They were researching into the cause of stomach ulcers. I washed bottles and drew pictures of microscopic slides for them. It paid £1 a week towards my lodgings, a fact I proudly announced in my next letter to Maurice. His reply was prompt:

> *I shall know where you are and what you are doing daily from 8 – 10. Eight o' clock is the time of our morning parade. The siren wakes us at 6.30. We are still under a roof and there is a small town not far away with nice, clean people, much different from the peasants in the south but somehow* die Lust ist hin, *I can't be bothered to make new acquaintances…*
>
> *I discovered a German hospital library in the Maternity Home! Hundreds of classics, and a lot by non-Fascist writers, even books by Kisch and Max Nordau. Obviously these books were dragged out of attics and cellars and nobody bothered to censor them. It is funny to think of soldiers unwittingly reading some Jewish authors – a crime worth a year or two in jug back in the Fatherland.*

Trust Maurice to find a hospital library to rifle, I thought. What a soldier's booty indeed! I told him how much Mrs Farlan and I enjoyed travelling with him through Italy.

> *My dear sweet,*
>
> *You are really very good with your letters. The last three are dated 2nd, 3rd and 5th of this month. It is good to think of you sitting in Martin's restaurant or awaiting a lecture or filling in time at home with a pen in your hand and talking to me across all that hostile space.*
>
> *And I reciprocate as far as the meagre ration of air letters allow. My surroundings are possibly more romantic. For instance, I am writing this lying on my bed which I have pitched under the tailboard of a lorry, a very good place indeed as the tailboard will protect me from the rain (but it will never rain, the weather is resplendent), and a hedge at the side keeps the breeze off and adds to the privacy of my nook. Added to this, I have all the delights of sleeping out in the open in such glorious weather. But I can see you frowning with perplexity – where is he? Alas, I cannot tell you, but I am no longer where I was!*

One advantage of moving is the amount of enforced leisure it gives you. I have plunged into the study of Turkish as a consequence and have made great progress.

We were sorely missed when we left the vicinity. We had supplied the population with food, salt (a very scarce commodity in Italy), work (our laundry) and – company! Some of our glamour boys had formed sentimental attachments and I still have to translate illiterate little missives in Italian, brought back by our despatch driver. The ladies are all very pious and usually wind up by saying that they are praying ardently to the Virgin Mary for the speedy return of the gentleman in question. And I believe they really do pray.

Once more I am out of books. I am a Don Juan with books! I think with longing of the London book markets – Farringdon St. for instance, for lovely, ancient, smelly tomes. Aren't you glad my passions are aroused only by such objects?

I looked up and saw that Mrs Farlan was stroking her cat and looking thoughtful.

"You are lucky, you know."

"What, with my husband in the army abroad, my brother in Palestine and my parents..."

"Oh, I am sorry. I meant with your husband. Does he wear a wedding ring?"

"No, why?"

"Well, I think it is a mistake that so many British men do not wear wedding rings." She got up, shook the cat off her lap and disappeared into the kitchen to prepare our cups of Horlicks.

I wondered if things were all right between her and her husband. She had started to bring home some of the classics from the library, which we now often discussed. Next day when I went scouring the second-hand book shops for Maurice, I came across one book which reminded me of my past work at the Lucas factory.

As you are reading novels now (why must you puzzle your brains over an outline of industrial practice?), I must tell you of a charming novel I have read. It is The Patriot *by Pearl Buck. A Chinaman goes to live in Japan, marries a*

Japanese girl but returns to China to fight for his country.
It is pleasantly written but pleased me most by its picture
of a doting married couple; they are very much in love
but of course the man spoils it all. Do read it! It will
interest you very much and awaken a little sympathy for
Japan. After all, it is the country where the wild cherry
comes from. Do you remember the intoxicating avenue in
Regents Park? No country with trees like those can be
entirely evil. I like Japanese poetry, it is brief. And they
have volcanoes, another charming trait. Anyhow, do
read the book and when you come to a passage I liked, I
know you'll stop and think of me.

Lying in this green valley and sleeping a perfumed
sleep, I can almost imagine myself in your arms. You
might be beside me, sketching the silhouette of two horses
on a hill or flirting with me outrageously.

Mrs Farlan made a note of 'The Patriot', and went to borrow it
from the library.

... I have two airmails from you dated the 2nd and 3rd...

I can't exchange any medical titbits, though you may
be interested to know that the old lady of the house I go
to has a heart complaint which apparently upset the renal
system and gives her oedematous legs. She needs
injections of mercurial diuretics and there are none to be
had. I scoured the city on my last visit to find some, but
there was absolutely nothing. So there you have one
more innocent victim of the war. Probably lots of people
are dying in this way for want of drugs.

Mrs Farlan and I commiserated over the suffering. The next part I
read in the privacy of my room.

... Don't you really think it tragic when Kony has to
declare that he had tried to be bitter after his girl's death,
but could only manage it for a week. How terrible it
would be if we could be as shallow in our emotions! I'd
rather suffer in the cruel way I do now because of our
separation, than take it calmly. Nothing I have done or
tried could fill one atom of the vacant place. I never
worry about the future as no future with you could see me

*unhappy. Twenty-four hours a day of each other's
company is the prospect that keeps me going and it is
worth while fighting my way across Europe to get it.*

I remembered Kony, his friend from his University days, who also
went to fight Franco. I was glad that they maintained contact.

As the exams drew nearer I tested myself and each time I got
something wrong my confidence would fall away. Maurice was always
reassuring me, as in the following letter:

*... Why get depressed when Frazer brings in a case and
you don't know the diagnosis? I bet it was something
once in a million. The fact is you were tired, overworked
and should have been resting. I envy you seeing* Jane
Eyre. *I've never seen Orson Welles act. And you lucky
girl, to be able to get acquainted with all these famous
novels without having to wade through enormous
Victorian tomes. Very useful for exams in English
literature. And the texts are usually good, as Hollywood
puts Aldous Huxley on the job. Naturally, the result was
not as good as* Pride and Prejudice. *Jane Austen is a
much greater author than Charlotte Bronte, but I bet the
film is better than the book.*

*The old lady with the oedema died suddenly. So I
think it must have been a cardiac condition. The family
will never be out of mourning. They had almost
completed mourning for a son who fell in Sicily.*"

Of course, it was uraemia and in my next letter Maurice got a
lecture on the subject.

A new anxiety arose at the beginning of June. There was a rumour
that all final exams for medical students would be cancelled in order to
draft them into hospitals to assist with anticipated casualties. 'D' Day
was being planned.

In fact, the Allies started the invasion on 6th June. However, the
exams proceeded and mine were fixed for the first week in July. It
was refreshing to read Maurice's happy letter which reached me in the
midst of my exam fever.

I read through the whole of Ignazio Silone's novel,
Fontamara, *in Italian in the course of a single day. My
dear, I beg you to note that this is a remarkable feat for a*

mere beginner and I expect your most flattering congratulations!

I am still pecking away at old Hogben's Interglossa. *Lucky man to be able to play around with such projects.*

I feel quite happy. It is now six months and more since I did a stroke of work so everything in the garden is lovely. I lead the life of a cultured man of leisure. I have my meals prepared for me; I stroll around the camp with half a dozen books under my arm; enjoy the respect and admiration of all and generally have a good time. You'll have a terrible time getting me to work again.

From this I knew his application for the interpreter's post in the intelligence corps must have failed. Neither of us ever mentioned it again.

Chapter Twenty-Four

Glasgow

This time the exams were to take place in Glasgow. I could not get there and back in one day. Mrs Farlan phoned around for a cheap room for one night and found one in a side street off Sauchiehall Street.

I arrived in the evening before the exams, too late for any supper and too late for a bath. The bath was full of soaking, dirty washing. I was starving. The landlady advised me to walk down to Sauchiehall Street. I gazed, puzzled, at the blacked-out road when a friendly policeman came up and asked me if I was lost. It was by now past 10 p.m.

"I am looking for a café. I have just arrived from Edinburgh and don't know the place." After a slight hesitation, I added: "A cheap café, where I can get a cup of tea and something to eat." The emphasis was on 'cheap'.

He looked down at me, then up and down the street and pointed to my right.

"Down there is a café open late."

I walked a few yards and came to the blue light above a blacked out glass door. I entered a smoke-filled room crowded with men. Spying a free table, I made straight for it. A man in rolled up shirtsleeves came up and I ordered a Welsh rarebit and tea.

At the table next to mine four men were holding an animated conversation. Every time they used a rude word – which I hardly understood – the man sitting nearest to my chair turned round and said: "Excuse us, lady." I gulped down my meal and left. I later discovered I had been directed to the unfashionable side of the famous street.

Next morning I ascended a steep hill to the maternity hospital and thought this climb might do for a natural induction for a woman at full term.

I completed my exams on 10th July and when I returned, Mrs Farlan greeted me with two letters from Maurice and a box of mixed nuts and almonds. She had got fresh eggs.

"No measly egg powder for us today," she smiled. I also got Lyons coffee and sumptuous cream buns to finish.

"I knew it in my bones that you would sail through it this time," she said, ignoring my plea to wait for the results in three days' time, when at 10.30 a.m. precisely the result would be posted up on the door of the Surgeon's Hall.

We sat chewing our feast, with her white cat purring at our feet. "Each kernel is a kiss from me," Maurice had written. How could I tell him about my blunder in Forensic Medicine?

"Why is suicide an offence in England and not in Scotland?" the examiner had asked when I thought the exam was over and he had leant back in his chair. I was puzzled as I could not remember coming across it in his textbook. I had waffled on about the higher regard for personal freedom in Scotland. Both examiners had smiled and said, "The law here is based on Roman Law."

This was a blow after I had answered every question correctly. Could they really fail me on this alone?

I eyed the still unopened letters from Maurice.

"Go on, open them, I know you are dying to," Mrs Farlan urged. I knew she was hoping for those titbits that I might read to her and so I did.

> ... The boys bring me copies of our propaganda leaflets in German to translate. The other day I had a chat with two German prisoners, mere lads of working class origin, about 19 years of age and definitely not Nazis. Quite happy. Our food is much better than theirs and as for our white bread... Their main preoccupation was whether they'd be sent to England or Canada.
>
> When I get home one of the first things I am going to do is to put you on top of the table and walk around it looking at you until I really know what you look like. And then I shall keep you on the mantelpiece and take you down every now and then. Would you like that? I wish I

had a miniature version of you in my breast pocket to look at.

I laughed as I told Mrs Farlan how Maurice had really sat me on the mantelpiece once in his study to settle a discussion on philosophy. The result had been a burnt dinner.

In the second letter Maurice made a surprising announcement:

> *... The die is cast! I have bought you – after much enquiry, searching and discrimination – a pretty little outfit in blue to go with your set. Yes, that is love indeed, me buying silk underwear! I shan't tell you the price, but it was definitely the pick of the bunch. Included in the parcel is a piece of Sardinian work – a table cover. I did not buy this, it was given to me as a souvenir by some very nice people in whose place we have been staying for the last few days and who fell in love with my Italian! So you see, the study of languages is justified; it has its practical uses.*

I realised that this was to be my wedding anniversary present in September.

Mrs Farlan was right. I had passed and was glad that for once I had not told Maurice of my fears after the exam. Now I allowed myself the extravagance and sent a telegram with the good news.

Chapter Twenty-Five

Graduation Day

On 20th July, 1944, a warm sunny Thursday morning, I awoke to hear Mrs Farlan singing in the kitchen,

"I'll take the High Road..."

The great day had arrived. I slipped into my dressing gown and was greeted in sing-song,

"And I've made you porridge and egg and toast. Have it while it's hot." She put this spread before me while she sat down to sip a cup of black tea.

"And where is *your* breakfast?" I asked.

"Can't have any. I'll have to wear my corset, which will be killing me but better dead than fat." She laughed. "Are you excited?"

"I'm not sure." I wondered if I should have to take the Hippocratic oath again.

I returned to my room to dress. On the table lay Maurice's letter, which had arrived the day before.

I shall try to peer through space at your graduation...

and further on I read as I sat at my dressing table:

I spent part of my siesta today (we have the siesta system now and are free to doze or read or go out from 12.30 – 4) reading a Penguin edition of Freud's Psycho-Pathology of Everyday Life *which treats the same material as the lectures we read together with so much enjoyment. It was our last intellectual adventure together after the stories of Keller, etc. Those glorious times when we read or studied together, delighting in each other's delight.*

And that is the formula for love; not only the pleasure of the individual but also the pleasure derived from the

knowledge that the beloved one is happy. And to think
that for a few years we were free to live together in such
a relationship in an atmosphere and world of our own.

I set my siestas apart for you; after I've written you a
letter, I get under the mosquito net and drowse and think
of you...
And then the gossamer sleep, the divine drowsiness of the
siesta, inimitable, there's a world of difference between it
and the heavy slumber of the night.

"The taxi is here!" Mrs Farlan shouted. I dabbed on some lipstick, grabbed my bag and we left. Mrs Farlan's sister was waiting in the taxi. At the station the porter showed us into a first class compartment.

Mrs Farlan, I noticed, sat very stiffly upright in a new flowered silk dress, to which I had contributed some coupons. She appeared to be several inches slimmer. Her sister, too, wore a silk outfit over which she had slung a silver fox fur; it now lay discarded beside her. Both wore new hats and white gloves, and shoes and bags in matching colours.

I was in my old blue Viennese silk suit which boasted, by a happy accident, a design of small pink flowers and leaves forming the 'V' sign and matching the pink georgette blouse. I had worn this outfit last in the Registrar's Office at my wedding. Alas, no Maurice at my side this time.

Mrs Farlan's sister had insisted on financing this treat: taxis, first class tickets to Glasgow and a table at a fashionable hotel-restaurant at the uppercrust end of Sauchiehall Street.

They had bought newspapers and presented me with the *Picture Post*, a lively weekly of the period which they knew I liked to read and send on to Maurice. They discussed the news about the advances of the Allies. I turned the pages of my journal, but my mind was not on it.

I had the strange feeling of being disembodied. It was my body only which sat there, which got up when we reached Glasgow, followed my companions to a taxi and did all that was required of it.

My mind leaped from the army tent in Italy to the kibbutz in Palestine. I tried to imagine what Maurice and my brother were doing at that precise moment.

Maurice, reading or filing to the accompaniment of nightingales singing – in broad daylight, as he had written the other week. How strange for the birds to be attracted by the racket of an army workshop in the middle of an Italian grove! Leo, in an orchard, picking oranges perhaps! I tried to remember when I had last tasted one. It must be very hot there now. Poor Leo! Had he fully recovered from his attack of Dengue Fever? This was the very illness I had intended to research had I been able to get an entry visa. How I had worked on my application, written in Hebrew, and sent to the University in Jerusalem! That was five years ago and still the virus was unknown. And my parents, where were they?

Then suddenly I found myself in the Great Hall.

When the ceremony started, I viewed the row of colleagues with me, mainly male. Some of them were already sporting brand new officer's uniforms. During the speeches they turned and smiled at their families and friends behind us.

I recalled my first graduation in Nazi-torn Vienna, in October 1938. My parents had rushed to the windows each time they heard a tram stop. They were afraid I might have been beaten up or seized as I came down the blood-stained great stairway of the classical facade of the university. When they saw me cross the street they waved and laughed and my brother came rushing down the stairs to meet me. In the sitting room my mother and father hugged me and I had to unfold the impressive document and translate the Latin text of the MD Vienna. This was disfigured, alas, by Nazi stamps which prohibited my practising in the great German Reich.

The speeches and the reading of the Hippocratic oath ended. I shook hands with the dignitaries, was given my scroll and returned to my two friends, for whose company I was grateful.

Another taxi took us to an expensive-looking Hotel-Restaurant where a special secluded table had been reserved. While the sisters discussed the menu I thought resentfully: why was it not my husband, my brother or my parents sitting there?

Where were my parents now? Leo had written that there was no hope of finding them still alive. My brain told me that they were dead, my heart still hoped for a miracle. No, I must stop these useless wrangles with my fate.

Mrs Farlan had removed the precious document from its cylinder mantle and unrolled the scroll.

I looked at the black Latin lettering and saw my married name in blue ink.   No more German name and no more German stamps forbidding me to practise at the very moment of my graduation.

It is a new beginning.   On Monday I start as locum for Dr MacNamara here in Edinburgh.   After six years of struggle, I am at last fully fledged to work in my profession.   That will be my true graduation.

Epilogue

We had to wait another nine months until Hitler obliged us with his death.

VE Day was celebrated with singing and dancing in the streets. Enthusiastic sounds of 'There'll always be an England...' and 'Land of Hope and Glory...' reverberated through the air. Bonfires were lit and fireworks exploded.

I was attending to casualties and dressing burns in the Derbyshire Children's Hospital. There, in Derby, Maurice found me on his return to this country. After his workshop had driven through Italy, he reached the south of Austria and got as far as Klagenfurth.

He had, however, another two years to complete four years' military service, which he spent in the Education Corps teaching reluctant boy soldiers in Woolwich. Their ardour to join the army had evaporated with the onset of peace. Schooling was not to their taste.

Maurice never spoke about his army experiences, which in his letters had often sounded like a Cook's tour. However, over the years I gathered that he had had a number of lucky escapes as their workshop was bombed and shelled on several occasions. He now longed to settle into a meaningful life.

Leo married and lived in Jerusalem where his son Herzel was born. He changed his own name in the Biblical style to the Hebrew 'son of his father's first name' – Ben Yehoshua.

Thus we had both shed our German names.

My parents were not as fortunate as their children. They were never to emerge alive from that God-forsaken village of Zasavica in Yugoslavia. The Red Cross was later to establish that the invading German Army had shot them there. This was some time in October, 1941. The Germans, so efficient in the completeness of their records of murders, omitted to note the date.

It was not until the end of 1946 that Maurice finally returned to me. I was then settled in Public Health in Huddersfield in Yorkshire. I worked in the Maternity and Child Welfare Clinics.

Maurice entered Leeds University where, a year later, he obtained a Diploma in Education. He then took up a post in a grammar school in Manchester, where he taught French and German to sixth form level. I applied for the first post I found advertised in the Manchester area and became Assistant County Medical Officer in Middleton on the fringe of Manchester.

There, in a cul-de-sac, Maurice found a semi-detached house with a back garden adjoining a bird sanctuary, with a small pond. We took on a substantial mortgage and became proud owner-occupiers.

As the removal men left we sank down on two tea chests in our future sitting-room, surrounded by boxes and piles of books, clutching the inevitable cups of tea. Looking out through the uncurtained window, we saw a robin redbreast who flew up to the window pane and picked at it – in greeting to us, or so we thought. It was of course his objection to his image in the glass which he had identified as a probable rival for his territory.

At dusk we went out into the back garden. A moorhen came out of the pond up on the ridge dividing our garden from the bird sanctuary to inspect the newcomers. Above us was a flock of rooks settling noisily into their high up nests in the tall elm trees for the night.

Around us autumn had started to paint the leaves with the first flush of red and gold. Maurice put his arm around my shoulders.

"For our tenth wedding anniversary we shall go to Italy: to Venice, Florence and Rome. This will be our belated honeymoon."

And that is exactly what we did.